“The funniest Danish novel I have read in a long time”
*Information*

“Satirically sharp and satirically funny”
*Weekendavisen*

“This is music to a language lover’s ears”
*Dagbladenes Bureau*, 5-star review

“Tremendously insightful”
*Jyllands-Posten*

“A poetic pearl”
*Berlingske Tidende*

“One of the best books I have read”
*LitteraturNu*

“Short, precise, and hugely entertaining”
*Litteratursiden*

Dorthe Nors was born in 1970 and is one of the most original voices in contemporary Danish literature. She holds a degree in literature and history from Aarhus University and has published four novels so far, in addition to the collection of stories and the novella you are holding in your hand. Nors's short stories have appeared in numerous publications, including *Harper's Magazine* and the *Boston Review*, and she is the first Danish writer ever to have a story published in the *New Yorker*. Nors was awarded the Danish Arts Agency's Three-Year Grant for "her unusual and extraordinary talent" in 2011. In 2014, *Karate Chop* won the prestigious P.O. Enquist Literary Prize.

# MINNA NEEDS REHEARSAL SPACE

Dorthe Nors

Translated from the Danish
by MISHA HOEKSTRA

Pushkin Press
71–75 Shelton Street, London WC2H 9JQ


Published by agreement with Ahlander Agency

*Minna Needs Rehearsal Space* was first published as
*Minna Mangler et Øvelokale* in Denmark in 2013



This edition first published by Pushkin Press in 2015

0 0 1

**DANISH ARTS FOUNDATION**

Grateful acknowledgment is made to the Danish Arts Council
and its Committee for Literary Project Funding and the Danish
Arts Agency for support in the writing and translation of the
book – and to Hald Hovedgaard for a writing residency.

ISBN 978 1 782271 19 2



Set in Sabon Monotype by Tetragon, London

Printed by CPI Group (UK) Ltd, Croydon CR0 4YY

www.pushkinpress.com

MINNA INTRODUCES HERSELF.

Minna is on Facebook.
Minna isn't a day over forty.
Minna is a composer.
Minna can play four instruments.
Minna's lost her rehearsal space.
Minna lives in Amager.
Minna spends her days in the Royal Library.
Minna has to work without noise.
Minna's working on a paper sonata.
The paper sonata consists of tonal rows.
Minna writes soundless music.
Minna is a tad avant-garde.
Minna has a tough time explaining the idea to people.
Minna wants to have sound with the music – no,
Minna just wants to have sound.
Minna wants to have Lars.
Minna's in love with Lars.
Lars used to really like Minna.
Minna doesn't dare click on the relationship app.
Lars has a full beard.
Lars has light-colored curls.
Lars works for the paper.
Lars is a network person.
*Lars is Lars*, Minna thinks, fumbling with the duvet cover.

It's morning.
Lars has left again.
Lars is always in a hurry to get out of bed.
The bed is a snug nest.
Minna's lying in it, but
Lars is on his bike and gone.
Lars bikes as hard as he can in the direction of City Hall Square.
Lars makes the pigeons rise.
Lars has deadlines.
Minna has an itch on her face.
Minna goes out to the bathroom to check.
Lars has kissed her.
Minna doesn't look like who she looked like when she made the spaghetti last night.
Minna looks like someone who drank all the wine herself.
Minna walks around in bare feet.
The flat is full of notes.
Bach stands in the window.
Brahms stands on the coffee table.
The flat's too small for a piano, but
A woman should have room for a flute.
A woman should have room for a flute, a triangle, and a guitar.
Minna takes out the guitar.
Minna plays something baroque.
Minna plays as quietly as possible.
The neighbor bangs on the wall with his sandals.
Minna needs a rehearsal space.
Minna needs security in her existence.
Minna misses the volume.
Minna misses a healthier alternative.

Minna wants to devote herself to ecology.
Minna wants to involve a kid in it.
Minna wants to try to be just like the rest.
Lars ought to help her but
Lars uses condoms.
Lars is on his bike and gone.
Lars is Lars.

*

Minna calls Lars.
Minna calls Lars until he picks up the phone.
Minna and Lars have discussed this before.
Lars has a cousin.
The cousin's name is Tim.
Tim knows of a rehearsal space in Kastrup.
The rehearsal space is close to the airport.
The rehearsal space is cheap.
Minna's never met Tim.
Minna is in many ways desperate.
Minna says, *I cannot keep on being quiet.*
Minna says, *I've got to be able to turn myself up and down.*
Lars sighs.
Minna says, *Let's bike out to the rehearsal space.*
Lars doesn't want to.
Lars is a culture reporter.
Lars and Minna met at a reception.
Lars introduced himself with his full name.
Minna could see that he knew everyone.
Minna could see that he would like to know everyone, but
Lars doesn't traffic in favors.

*Favors are for politicians*, he says.
Minna says, *But it's just a rehearsal space.*
Lars says, *One day it's rehearsal space, the next . . .*
The conversation goes on like that.
Minna pesters.
Lars relents, but only a little.
Lars says that he can call up Tim.
Minna waits by the phone.
Minna changes an A string.
Minna drinks her coffee.
The phone doesn't ring.
Minna goes for a walk.
The phone doesn't ring.
The phone is dead.
Minna checks the SIM card.
The SIM card's working.
Amager Strandpark is shrouded in sea fog.
Amager Strandpark is full of architect-designed bunkers.
Amager Strandpark wants to look like Husby Dunes.
Husby Dunes used to be part of the Atlantic Wall.
Husby Dunes used to be a war zone.
Amager Strandpark makes itself pretty with a tragic backdrop.
Minna doesn't like Amager Strandpark.
Minna really likes the Sound.
Minna loves the sea, the gulls, the salt.
Minna is a bit of a water person, and now her pocket beeps.
Minna looks at her cellphone.
Lars has sent a text.
*Tim's on Bornholm*, it says.
Minna was prepared for something like that, but

Minna wasn't prepared for what comes next:
Lars writes, *I think we should stop seeing each other.*
Minna reads it again, but that's what it says.
Lars is breaking up with a text.
Minna cannot breathe.
Minna has to sit down on an artificial dune.
Minna writes, *Now I don't understand.*
Minna calls on the phone.
There's no signal.
Minna waits for an answer.
The cell is dead, and so she sits there:
Amager Strandpark is Husby Dunes meets Omaha Beach.
Amager Strandpark is full of savage dogs trying to
flush something out.
Amager Strandpark is a battlefield of wounded women.

*

Minna has gotten Lars to elaborate on his text.
Lars has written, *But I'm not really in love with you.*
Lars has always understood how to cut to the chase.
Minna can't wring any more out of him.
Lars is a wall.
Lars is a porcupine.
Minna lies in bed.
The bed's the only place she wants to lie.
Minna hates that he began the sentence with *But*.
Minna feels that there was a lot missing before *But*, but
Minna should have apparently known better.
Men are also lucky that they possess the sperm.
Men can go far with the sperm.

Men with full sacks play hard to get.
Men with full sacks turn tail, but
Minna can manage without them.
Minna's a composer.
Minna feels her larynx.
The larynx isn't willing.
Minna can hear her neighbor come home.
Minna places an ear against the wall.
The neighbor dumps his groceries on the table.
The neighbor takes a leak.
Minna puts Bach on the stereo.
Minna turns up Bach.
The neighbor is there instantly.
Bach's cello suites are playing.
Minna's fingers are deep in the wound.
Minna looks at the portrait of Lars.
The portrait's from the paper.
Lars is good at growing a beard.
Lars sits there with his beard.
Lars's mouth is a soft wet brushstroke.
Chest hair forces his T-shirt upward.
The beard wanders downward away from his chin.
An Adam's apple lies in the middle of the hair.
Minna's had it in her mouth.
Minna's tasted it.
Minna's submitted, but
Lars looks out at someone who's not her.
Lars regards his reader.
It's not her.
Minna's tormenting herself.

Minna feels that Lars is a hit-and-run driver.
The hit-and-run driver has suffered at most a dented fender.
Minna savors her injuries.
Her heart is spot bleeding.
Her mouth stands agape.
Minna comforts herself.
Minna has the music, after all.
No one can take the music from her.
The music's an existential lifeline.
Minna would just rather have a child.
Minna ought to be glad for what she's got.
Minna would just rather have a child.
Once upon a time, composers were sufficient unto themselves.
Composers didn't need to have children.
The tendency has changed:
Minna should take it upon herself to have a child.
Minna looks at the bookcase.
Minna grabs the first book under B.
Ingmar Bergman opens up for her.
Bergman's wearing the beret.
Bergman's gaze peers deep into Minna.
Bergman wants to get in under Minna's persona.
Minna's persona attempts to make way for him.
Minna wants Bergman all the way inside.
Bach plays.
The neighbor thumps.
Bergman drills.
Minna keeps all superfluous organs to the side.
Bergman says, *I drill, but . . .*
*The drill breaks, or else I don't dare drill deep enough.*

Minna's managed the impossible:
Bergman can't find the woman in Minna.
The mother won't turn up.
The mother, the whore, the witch.
Minna lifts up her blouse a little.
Bergman shakes his head.
Minna stuffs him up under the blouse.
Bergman doesn't protest.
Bergman makes himself comfortable.
Bergman whispers sweet words to her.
Bergman's words don't work.
Minna's lower lip quivers.
Minna whispers, *I used to sing*.

*

Minna hasn't been out of her flat in three days.
Minna's sent a lot of texts.
Minna's asked Lars to tell her what was supposed to be in front of *But*.
Lars doesn't reply.
Lars won't budge an inch.
Lars was otherwise so mellow.
Minna recalls when they last saw each other.
Minna and Lars lay in bed.
Minna stroked his beard.
Minna read and interpreted.
Lars just needs time.
Minna decides to send Lars an email.
Minna writes, *I think we should meet and talk about it.*
Minna writes, *We can always of course be friends.*

Minna writes, *I miss you so*.
It's wrong to write that, yet she's written it regardless.
It thunders through the ether.
The email's directional.
Minna's ashamed.
The rehearsal space is gone.
Tim's on Bornholm.
Minna's got no money.
Minna's got no boyfriend.
Minna's got only herself, and now she's going out.
Minna goes down the stairs.
Minna goes down to her bike.
The bike stands in the backyard.
The backyard amplifies all sound.
The neighbors' orgasms, the magpies, the pigeons dominate.
Minna puts on her bike helmet.
Minna bikes onto Amagerbrogade.
Minna walks through the revolving doors into the Royal Library.
Minna wants to concentrate.
The young female students are wearing high heels.
The heels bang against the floor.
Minna despises the students' high heels.
Minna despises their catwalk character.
Minna doesn't think they've studied what they ought to.
Minna fiddles with her sonata.
Minna picks long hairs from her blouse.
Minna waits for news from Lars.
Karin's sent her an email.
Karin sends lots of emails every day.

Karin's emails are long.
Karin tells about her life in the country.
Minna's with her in the bedroom.
Minna's with her at handball in the gym.
Minna isn't shielded from anything.
Karin uses Minna as a diary.
Karin's everyday life will take over Minna's.
Minna makes a rare quick decision.
Minna writes, *Dear Karin.*
*It's not you.*
*It's me.*
Minna breaks up with Karin.
*All things must have an end.*
*A worm has two.*
Minna doesn't write that last bit.
One shouldn't hurt others unnecessarily.
One should above all be kind.
Minna would rather not be anything but.
Minna's hardly anything but.
The email thunders through the ether toward Karin.
*That's as it should be*, thinks Minna.
The ether is full of malicious messages.
The ether hums with break-ups and loss.
The ether is knives being thrown.
The ether is blood surging back.
Minna has wounded a creature.
Minna stares out on the canal.
Minna listens to the banging heels.
Minna needs to go to the bathroom.

*

Minna's peed.
Minna's back in her place.
Minna sits and feels the pain.
The pain's a contagion.
The borders recede.
Cynicism buds.
*Pointlessness grimaces!*
Minna's snuck Bergman out of her bag.
Minna's got to concentrate.
Someone waves from behind the panoramic glass.
Jette's standing with a bakery bag.
Coffee's to be drunk on the quay.
Jette's a classically trained harpist.
Jette's given up finding rehearsal space.
The harp's stood in the way her entire life.
Minna knows the feeling.
Minna's had the same experience with grand pianos, but
Grand pianos grow on trees.
Harps are exclusive.
Harps are for fairies, angels, and the frigid.
Jette's erotic.
Jette calls her boyfriends *lovers*.
Jette's boyfriends are married to other women.
Jette's studying composition in Reading Room North.
Minna writes paper sonatas in Reading Room East.
Minna and Jette drink coffee together.
The relationship isn't supposed to get serious.
Jette talks too much about bodies.
Jette has an IUD in her genital tract.
Jette has discharges and domestic obligations.

Jette needs a weekend escape with a lover.
Jette fears vaginal dryness.
The uterus is an abandoned studio flat.
The vagina's the gateway to the enjoyment of all things.
Jette says, *Don't you agree?*
Minna says, *Isn't that a balloon?*
Minna points to a spot above the harbor.
Jette's content with the two kids she has.
*Enough's enough*, says Jette.
*Jette has two kids*, thinks Minna.
Minna has a hard time getting up from the quay.
Minna feels like a horse.
Minna says, *I think it was Bugs Bunny.*
Jette goes through the door into the Royal Library.
Minna stands there like a fly in the ointment, and then she has to pee.
Minna has to really pee, and it has to happen fast.

*

Minna has to go to the john twice a day on average when she works at the Royal Library.
Minna pees.
Minna fills her water bottle from the tap.
Minna leaves the john.
Minna's surrounded by a couple hundred police officers in mufti.
The officers are with the Danish National Police.
The officers stand at attention in the buffet area.
The officers are at a conference in the Karen Blixen Meeting Room.
Minna watches the deputy commissioner eat a fish roll.
Minna slopes through the crowd.

Minna's a relic.
Minna spools up across two hundred officers.
Minna towers over four hundred sperm-filled sacs.
The officers' laughter bursts through the room.
Jens Peter Jacobsen shudders.
Hans Christian Andersen ditto.
Yard upon yard of shelving turns its back.
Minna writes tonal rows.
Minna sweats.
Minna works like a horse.
Minna heaves the tones around on the paper.
Minna clears her throat.
Minna clears her throat a little more.
The girl to her left shushes her.
Minna packs up and rides downstairs.
Minna enters the revolving doors from one side.
A police officer enters from the other.
Minna revolves around with the officer.
Minna is walking and going round.
The revolving door mechanism feels defective.
The officer gets his foot caught.
The revolving door stops heavily.
The revolving door spits Minna out like a clay pigeon.
Iceland Wharf lies far beneath Minna.
Iceland Wharf shines flat and practical.
Minna sees far beneath her the mermaid on the quay.
Minna looks out across the city.
Minna floats.
Minna's in flight over Copenhagen.
Minna's an instance of female buoyancy and helium.

*

Lars is as silent as the grave, but
Karin's answered quickly.
Minna's seated herself in her kitchen at home.
Minna doesn't dare open the email from Karin.
Karin plays accordion.
Minna and Karin took a class together.
Karin latched on to Minna.
Minna is somewhat of a host species.
Minna has now finally told Karin to stop.
The decision's good enough.
The decision was just made too late.
Karin feels bad now.
Karin's self-worth has been damaged.
Karin's self-worth is Jutlandic.
Karin brags about motocross, sex, and pork sausage.
Karin's married to a farmer.
The farmer's bought up the parish.
The parish belongs to Karin.
Karin drinks tall boys.
Karin plays folk dances.
Karin's on the gym board.
Karin sticks her hand all the way up her neighbor.
Karin grasps the inner udder.
Karin milks.
Karin pinches and squeezes.
The teat yields.
The teat's tugged long and white.
The teat grows tender and stiff.
The teat grows so tired in the end.

Minna also wrote her, *Now relax*, but
Karin doesn't need to restrain herself:
Karin goes to zumba.
Minna was right to break up with her.
A person ought to defend herself.
Minna opens the email from Karin.
Minna's right.
Karin writes nasty things about Minna.
Minna can't for instance land a man.
Men don't want women like Minna.
*Age will drag you down!!!* Karin writes.
*Barrenness will haunt you!!!* Karin writes, and continues:
Minna doesn't know how to live.
Minna only knows how to think.
Karin's got everything that Minna wants.
Karin's got a dog, a man, and kids.
Karin's got 500 acres of land.
Minna's got zilch.
Minna's lonely, a failure, and deserves to be pissed on.
Karin pisses.
Minna thinks that should suffice.
People are getting worse and worse.
Middle fingers poke out of car windows.
Small dogs shit before her entryway.
Young men shout *whore*.
The three Billy Goats Gruff play havoc in nice folks' sunrooms.
People's faces look kind.
People's faces *aren't* kind.
Minna wants to reply.
Minna wants to write nasty things too, but

Minna thinks enough's enough.
Minna longs for shut traps.
Minna longs for stillness and beauty.
Minna seats herself by the window.
Minna looks down on the street.
Minna watches a tiny dog back up to the curbstone and gently squeeze out a turd.

*

Night has descended on Amager.
Denmark is laid in darkness.
The Sound flows softly.
The planes take off and land.
Minna awakens.
Minna gasps.
Lars was in the dream.
Minna and Lars were at the beach.
Minna was buried with just her head free.
The sea was rough at the foot of the dune.
The sea raged, foaming white.
Dad stood in the breakers and waved.
Minna wanted to grab Lars in her haste.
Minna wriggled her arms.
The arms wouldn't budge.
Lars pelted her with sand.
Lars patted her hard with a shovel.
Lars poured water over her.
Lars used her to build a sandcastle.
The wave reached land.
The wave reached land and trickled slowly.

The beads of gravel rattled.
Dad vanished.
Minna awoke.
Minna turned on the light, and now it is quiet.
Amager steams with rain.
The rain refracts off the manholes.
Minna never bakes cake.
Minna gets up to bake a cake.
Minna bakes a cake in the middle of the night.
Cake is the opiate of the people.

*

Jette sits on the quay and is intimate.
Minna's brought cake for coffee.
Minna unwraps the tinfoil from a piece of cake.
The tinfoil feels childish.
The cake isn't very good either.
Jette's been to a seminar.
Jette has a new lover.
The lover's Russian.
The Russian's as hot as fresh borscht.
The Russian's French is good.
*Jette's got Reds in her pleasure pavilion*, thinks Minna.
Minna looks at the mermaid on the quay.
The mermaid is green.
The mermaid cannot swim.
The mermaid would sink to the bottom immediately.
Minna says, *Such sun!*
Jette says, *What about you?*
Minna says, *I'm working on the paper sonata.*

Minna knows perfectly well that Jette means sex.
Minna knows perfectly well that Jette wants to trade moisture.
Minna knows perfectly well that Jette's leading on points.
Karin too.
Minna understands completely.
It's something to do with physics.
It's something to do as well with the soul.
Minna can't explain it.
Minna bloody won't explain it either.
Minna looks at the mermaid.
The mermaid's tailfin is cast in bronze.
The mermaid's tailfin can't slap.
The world is a suit of clothes.
The clothes too tight.
The corneas drying out.
Minna stretches: *Work calls.*
Jette says, *Leaving already?*
Minna is.
Minna disappears up to the reading room.
Minna stares at her inbox.
*Everyone writes and no one answers*, thinks Minna.
Elisabeth's written.
Elisabeth will treat her to a cup of tea.
Elisabeth is Minna's big sister.
*Karin, Elisabeth, and Jette*, thinks Minna.
*Women in their prime.*
*Women with the right to vote.*
*Women with educations.*
*Women with their own needs.*
*Women with herb gardens and the pill.*

*Steamrollers*, thinks Minna.
One mustn't think like that.
*Women are awful to women*, Minna's mother's always said.
Mom's right, but
Women are tough to swallow.
Minna doesn't understand why men like women.
Women want to cross the finish line first.
Women want to look good on the podium.
Women are in the running, but
Minna's otherworldly.
Minna's a composer.
Minna's not a mother.
Minna doesn't have a mothers' group.
Minna sees the mothers' group often.
The mothers' group takes walks in Amager.
The mothers' group drives in formation.
The mothers' group is scared of getting fat.
The mothers' group goes jogging with their baby buggies.
The mothers' group eats cake at the café.
The mothers' group contends gently for the view.
The baby buggies pad the façade.
The baby buggies form a breastwork.
Minna fears the mothers' group.
Minna cannot say that out loud.
Minna doesn't have a child.
Minna can't let herself say anything.
Minna's not home free.
Minna once won a prize for some chamber music.
Minna would rather have gotten a license to live.

*

Minna's laid herself down on the couch.
Minna looks forward:
The prospect's hazy.
Minna looks backward:
Time has passed.
Minna recalls the Bay of Aarhus.
Minna recalls Dad:
Dad and Minna hike through Marselisborg Forest.
Dad and Minna hike down to Ballehage Beach.
Dad and Minna sniff the anemones.
Dad and Minna change into their bathing suits.
Dad and Minna position themselves on the pier.
Dad and Minna inhale the salt.
The wind's taken hold of Dad's hair.
The wind whips round Minna's ditto.
Dad and Minna stand with arms extended.
Dad's armpits hairy.
Minna's bathing suit with balloon effect.
Dad's finger toward the horizon: *Helgenæs!*
Minna takes a running jump.
Minna shoots out into the bay.
Dad's a water bomb.
Dad and Minna dive.
Dad and Minna splash each other.
Dad and Minna can do anything, but
Minna grew up.
Minna had to bathe alone.
Minna hiked through Marselisborg Forest.
Minna wanted to hike down to Ballehage, but
Minna met a roe deer.

The deer stood on a bluff.
The deer stood stock-still and stared at Minna.
Minna stood stock-still and stared at the deer.
The deer was a creature of the deep forest.
The deer was mild and moist of gaze.
Minna was mild and moist of gaze.
The deer's legs like stalks.
The deer's fur in the sun.
Minna's hair in the wind.
The forest was empty when the deer departed.
Minna looked across the bay.
Minna inhaled the salt.
Minna gazed at the pier.
Minna picked mushrooms from half-rotted stumps.
Minna threw her arms around a beech tree.
Love ought to find its voice again.
Loss ought to fade out, but
*Loss and love are connected*, Minna thinks.
Minna lies in Amager.
Minna turns on her side.
*Love presupposes loss.*
Minna deeply misses Lars.
The pain's connected to hope.
Hope is light green.
Hope's a roe deer on a bluff.
*Someone has got to love*, thinks Minna.
*Someone's got to fight.*

*

Minna's got a lot to fight.
Lars has deleted her.
Minna's no longer friends with Lars.
Lars has spoken.
Minna's been expunged.
Lars has disappeared from her wall, but
Minna can see Lars everywhere.
Lars hangs out with the others.
Lars invites people for beer.
That's awful enough.
This is worse:
Lars comments on everything Linda Lund says.
Linda Lund also attended the conservatory.
Minna was good at piano.
Linda was good at guitar, but
Linda's better suited to the music industry.
Minna can screw a reporter and still not get her picture in the paper.
Linda Lund's just got to cross the street.
Linda's sex appeal is undeniable.
Minna can feel Linda's sex in everything.
Sex is power.
Sex is currency.
Linda is loaded.
The world's a stage.
The stage is Linda's.
No one may block the view of Linda.
Minna knows that.
Minna and Linda run into each other now and then.
Minna's still got scars from the last time.

Minna stood there with her score.
Minna was making for the stage.
Minna was supposed to perform just like the others, but
Minna ran into Linda in the wings.
Linda pulled out a mental machete.
Linda slashed a couple times.
Linda said, *That dress will blend into the curtain.*
Linda said, *What's your name again?*
Minna almost couldn't perform afterward.
Lars is in a fix.
Lars congratulates Linda on her birthday.
Linda replies, *Thanks for last night, kiss kiss.*
Lars writes, *Nice!*
Linda says, *It certainly was.*
Lars says, *Rock on, babe!*
Linda's a cannonball in jacket and skirt.
Lars is a hypnotized reporter.
Minna sits and gasps.
Karin sits on the grill of her 4 x 4.
Karin sits and smiles on her 4 x 4.
Minna unfriends vehicle and Karin both.
Minna unfriends Linda Lund too.
Minna doesn't want to be an unwilling witness!
Minna doesn't want her nose rubbed in the piss.
Minna unfriends another two people.
Minna unfriends more.
Minna unfriends Britta.
Britta's an old schoolmate.
Britta's written,
*Britta's put the pork loin on the Weber.*

Minna can no longer leave well enough alone, but
The unfriendings provide no relief.
Minna's been unfriended herself.
The pain of unfriending's unbearable.
Minna misses Lars.
Lars has inflicted a trauma.
Minna's in love with someone who's traumatized her.
Minna reckons that makes her a masochist.
Minna doesn't want to be a masochist.
Minna wants to be a human being, but
Minna's expunged.
*It hurts so much*, Minna whispers.
Minna goes into the shower.
Minna lets the water run, and then she stands there:
Minna with her lips turned toward the tiles.
Minna with blood on her hands.
Minna with soap in her eyes.
Minna with no roe deer.

*

*The ringmaster of a flea circus lets the artists suck his blood.*
Bergman strokes Minna on the cheek.
*A daydreamer isn't an artist except in his dreams.*
Bergman reaches for the buttermilk.
Bergman has indigestion.
Minna has a burnt taste in her mouth.
Bergman whispers, *I contain too much humanity.*
*The days are long, large, light.*
*They're as substantial as cows, as some sort of bloody big animal.*
Minna snuggles up to Bergman.

Dad strokes Minna's cheek.
Dad settles himself on his rock.
Dad understands.
Dad isn't scared.

*

Minna's read Bergman for a couple days.
Minna's tired of lying in bed.
Minna checks her email.
Minna's gotten lots of email.
Mom and Jette have written.
Elisabeth's written, and look here:
Karin's written.
That was expected.
Minna doesn't know if she'll read Karin's missive.
The street clatters with bikes and cars.
The sun's risen over Amager Strandpark.
Baresso's opened.
The coffees to go are warming palms.
The coffees to go are out walking.
The cellphones, the blankies, the coffees to go.
People trickle toward City Hall Square.
People look like shoals of shiny herring.
People press on with sand and sleep in their eyes.
Minna eats a cracker.
Karin's missive awaits.
Karin wants to be nasty.
Karin wants to upset her applecart, but
Minna's cart has no apples.
The damage has been done.

Lars has disappeared.
Linda's getting laid.
Karin's got a dog.
Karin takes walks with her dog on the beach.
The dog'll fetch a stick for Karin.
The dog whips back and forth.
Karin throws farther and farther.
The dog doesn't hold back.
Karin casts the stick into the ocean.
The dog throws itself in.
Karin keeps casting the stick.
The dog keeps bounding.
It could continue this way forever, but
Minna's got to get to it.
Minna reads:
Karin's discovered that she's been unfriended.
Karin's hurt.
Karin repeats the gist from last time.
Karin just spices the gist up a bit:
*Jutland women can fuck!!!*
*Music should be popular!!!*
*Music shouldn't be deep!!!*
*KARIN LOVES BRYAN ADAMS!!!*
Minna swallows her cracker.
Karin keeps going: *I feel bad for you!!!*
Karin can say more: *You'll come to regret it!!!*
Minna's counted Karin's exclamation points.
The email contains fifty-six exclamation points.
That's plenty, but
Minna doesn't even feel like crying.

Minna's anesthetized to blows.
Minna looks out the window.
Minna looks down upon the transport tsunami.
The network people whizz away.
The network people have got business cards.
A chink suffices.
The darkness yields willingly, but
Network hearts don't have the time.
Minna considers her hands.
Minna thinks her hands resemble thimbles.
Minna's hands *are* thimbles.
Thimbles can't grab.
The world around is laid with tile.
Network people are highly polished.
Minna shakes herself.
Minna tests her grasping power on her hair.
Her fingers can still grab herself hard.
*Better than nothing*, thinks Minna, and sits down.

*

Paper sonatas don't write themselves.
Minna bikes to the Royal Library.
The city's blazing hot from the sun.
The cell's blazing hot from messages.
Elisabeth's after her.
Elisabeth's ten years older than Minna.
Elisabeth's married to a successful optician.
Elisabeth lives in the Potato Row Houses.
The optician's skinny and dry.
Minna understands him.

The optician's a guest in his own home.
Guests have it rough at Elisabeth's.
Shoes have to be taken off in the hallway.
Shoes must never cross the threshold.
The guest has to pee.
The guest really has to pee.
The john lies on the far side of the utility room.
The shoes have to be removed anyway.
The shoes have to be put on and taken off without leaning on the walls.
The walls in the hallway must not get grime spots.
The bench in the hallway must not have any bottoms upon it.
The bench is *not* to sit on.
The bench is there to create harmony in the hallway.
The guest is barefoot and entering a house full of rules.
Elisabeth makes the rules.
No one else has permission to make rules in the house.
Cutlery must not clink against the service.
The table must not be wiped with a wet rag.
Books must be bound in dust jackets.
Fingers must not touch the pictures.
The coffee mugs must not stand without coasters underneath.
The coffee mugs must not contain coffee.
Coffee is forbidden at Elisabeth's.
Everyone must drink tea.
The optician gets the trots from tea, but
The optician must remove his shoes before he runs to the john.
The optician struggles with his suede shoes in the hallway.
The optician's afraid to place his fingers anywhere.
The optician just reaches the toilet in his stocking feet.

The shit runs out of him like green tea.
Elisabeth shouts, *Is that you, honey?*
The shit runs and runs.
The optician considers whether he dares to shit any more.
Elisabeth shouts, *Is that you who came home, honey?*
The optician reaches for the toilet paper.
The optician remembers to tear it off in a straight line.
The optician's lonesome, completely without allies.
Elisabeth and the optician have neither dog nor kids.
It's sad, but
One thing is certain:
Kids set their bottoms everywhere.
Elisabeth's turning fifty besides.
Elisabeth's still pretty.
Elisabeth's hair is fair like Minna's, but
Elisabeth's hair doesn't dare curl.
Elisabeth is illuminated.
Elisabeth is an act of will.
Elisabeth's sent Minna a stream of messages.
Minna sits on her bike and reads them.
Minna approaches Knippel Bridge.
Minna has one hand on the handlebars.
Minna has one eye on the display.
Elisabeth wants her to phone.
Elisabeth wants her to drop by.
Minna passes the Stock Exchange.
Minna holds for a bus.
Minna MUST ring between two and four.
Minna MUST NOT ring at any other time.
Elisabeth practices yoga and meditates.

The day is scheduled.
Elisabeth says it's all about respecting others' needs.
Minna understands:
Lars has a need to screw a celebrity.
Jette has a need to share her sex life.
Karin has a need to take up space out in the country.
Linda Lund has a need for an audience.
Minna has to get up to stand on the pedals.
Minna is honked at.
Minna bikes out into the intersection by the Stock Exchange.
Elisabeth pursues her.
Elisabeth was an only child for ten years.
Elisabeth's still an only child.
Elisabeth isn't healthier than Karin.
Karin requires a host animal.
Elisabeth requires weak creatures.
Weak creatures can defer their needs.
Elisabeth has to be done with hers first.
Elisabeth will never be done with hers.
Elisabeth was never at Ballehage Beach either.
The sand was a mess, but
Dad and Minna could dive.
Minna's not weak.
Minna won't!
The traffic roars around Minna.
The traffic's unsafe.
Minna turns past Det Røde Palæ.
Minna bikes and taps.
Minna taps, *I'm just on my bike.*
Elisabeth orders her to call anyway.

Minna turns off her cell.
Minna drops the cell into her bag.
The bag trembles in the bike basket.
Minna trembles on the bike, but
Paper sonatas don't write themselves.

*

The quay oozes female students.
The police officers are back in Karen Blixen.
The officers stand smoking on the quay.
The officers keep an eagle eye on the students.
The students don't see the officers.
The students cast their hair about.
Their hair flips from side to side.
The students get to their feet.
The officers get to their feet.
The students' legs grow long.
The officers' pants have pockets.
The officers tug at their pockets.
The officers camouflage their sperm-filled bits.
Minna and Jette sit *sans camouflage* in the midst of it all.
Jette's eyes are insistent.
Minna has a hard time relaxing.
The legs biking.
The arms warding off blows.
The body full of vim.
The soul supposed to sit still.
It ain't easy.
Jette notices that sort of thing.
Jette says, *You seem stressed out*.

Minna replies, *I've got a little too much going on.*
Jette says, *Tell, tell!*
Minna says, *Oh, you know . . .*
Jette says, *You shouldn't walk around keeping everything bottled up.*
Minna says, *The paper sonata's bumping along.*
Minna says that she'll buy a keyboard.
Jette thinks she could just use her Mac.
Macs have a program for composers.
Macs are easy to figure out.
Minna doesn't want to say that she can't figure them out.
Minna doesn't want to satisfy Jette's need to know better.
Minna says, *It's my sister, that's all.*
Minna points at the mermaid on the quay.
The mermaid by the Royal Library is prettier than Langelinie's.
The mermaid by the Royal Library is anything but charming.
The mermaid by the Royal Library can do somersaults.
The mermaid has just come ashore.
The quay is a rock.
The mermaid has a hold, but
The world makes it tough.
Anne Marie Carl-Nielsen made the mermaid.
Anne Marie Carl-Nielsen was kind to animals.
Anne Marie Carl-Nielsen was married to Carl Nielsen.
Anne Marie Carl-Nielsen was a great sculptor.
Carl Nielsen was a great composer.
*Carl Nielsen wasn't an easy man to be married to*, says Minna.
*Carl Nielsen couldn't ignore his needs.*
Carl was a firecracker.
Carl was a billy goat.

Anne Marie sculpted horses in Jutland.
Carl had ladies visit in Copenhagen.
Anne Marie's horses got bigger and bigger.
Carl's ladies got rifer and rifer.
Anne Marie placed herself beneath the horses.
Carl placed himself beneath the ladies.
Anne Marie had to learn to forgive.
Anne Marie had to stomach it.
The mermaid casts herself up out of the sea.
The mermaid contracts like a muscle before it explodes.
The mermaid clings to dry land, angry and insecure.
The mermaid is pure wet will.
She gasps.
She stares at the quay's young people.
*Carl Nielsen was a handsome man*, says Jette.
*Carl Nielsen was stumpy*, says Minna.
*Carl Nielsen could've been my lover*, says Jette.
The conversation's taken a familiar turn.
The Russian has a wife in Moscow.
The wife in Moscow doesn't know a thing.
Minna looks at the mermaid.
The mermaid knows all.

*

Minna's mother lives in Aarhus.
Minna's from Jutland, just like Karin.
Minna's just not from Jutland in the same way.
Minna's from Marselisborg Forest.
Minna's an old man's daughter.
Minna's a younger widow's caboose.

Mom's still a widow, but
Mom's got a boyfriend.
The boyfriend's name is Finn.
Finn and Mom go to museums.
Finn and Mom attend folk high school.
Finn and Mom each live alone.
Mom's too old for the whole package.
Finn would otherwise be interested, but
Mom's master in her own home.
Mom's also good at staying in touch.
Mom's taken a computer class at the Senior Club.
Mom's on Facebook.
Mom's got a blog.
Mom can text.
*Elisabeth says you're feeling poorly*, she writes.
*Elisabeth's worried*, she writes.
Mom's worried too.
Minna stands in the hallway and reads.
Minna considers getting a cat.
The cat'd come stealing in from the living room.
The cat'd rub up against Minna's leg.
*The cat and Bergman*, Minna thinks.
Minna collapses on the couch.
Bergman rests on the table.
Bergman's there for the grasping.
*You'll do what's needed*, he says.
*Failures can have a fresh, bitter taste*, he says.
Minna lays him to her breast.
Bergman makes himself at home there.
Minna closes her eyes:

Minna can hear the cars down on the street.
Minna can hear herself drawing breath.
Bergman curls up into a ball.
Minna dozes off.
Minna dreams of a house on a hill.
The yard bulges with fruit and lilacs.
Phlox, mallow, iris blossoming.
The gable wall glows with English roses.
The fjord flashes at the foot of the hill.
Minna's seated on the patio.
The boats tack into the wind.
The henhouse has been whitewashed.
The henhouse is the rehearsal space.
The grand piano stands plumb in the middle.
Minna turns her face toward the sun.
Minna's chest arches over her heart.
The heart is lovely in its dissolution.
The heart has weathered the storm.
Minna listens to the interior of the house.
The door's opened and shut.
Keys are laid upon the table.
Someone's approaching the patio door.
Lars stands there smiling.
Lars bends over his woman.
Lars caresses his woman's belly.
The baby kicks inside.
The reaper-binder rattles outside.
The skylarks sing high in the air.
The rifle club's meeting in the gravel pit.
The rifle club shoots clay pigeons.

The clay pigeons whizz across the landscape.
The clay pigeons are shot or shatter when they fall.
The clay pigeons fall and fall.
Minna's wakened by a muffled thud on the floor.
It's Bergman.
It's Monday, Minna remembers.
She's in Amager, she remembers.

*

It's a miracle.
Elisabeth's visiting Minna's flat.
Elisabeth stands in the middle of the living room.
Elisabeth's in stocking feet.
The face as hard as enamel.
Elisabeth's rage is a legend in the family.
The examples are legion:
Elisabeth removes bikes in Potato Row.
Nothing may shade the house.
Nothing may destroy the harmony of the façade.
Elisabeth doesn't move the bikes a couple yards.
Elisabeth walks around to other streets with the bikes.
No one should think they're safe.
Elisabeth threatens people with lawsuits and psychotic episodes.
Elisabeth drives people to numerologists, and even worse:
Elisabeth once made Mom have a breakdown over a piece of royal porcelain.
Elisabeth's aligned the stars on her side, and now she stands in the living room:
Dust rises: *Didn't I tell you to call?*
Elisabeth continues, *Didn't I tell you to come by?*

Minna proffers tea.
Elisabeth sets her purse down on the coffee table.
Elisabeth's eyes flit from the dirty laundry to Bach.
Elisabeth's eyes need to shut for a bit.
Minna edges past her sister.
Minna pours calcified water into two mugs from IKEA.
Minna stuffs in the teabags.
Minna walks back to the living room.
Elisabeth has seated herself.
Minna sets a mug before her.
Elisabeth doesn't want the tea.
The tea ought to be green, *And why didn't you call me then?*
Minna doesn't manage to answer.
Elisabeth cranks up the language.
The language lashes Minna.
The language is a castigation.
Minna sips her tea.
*Sisters should be there for each other*, Elisabeth says.
*Sisters should save each other from the muck.*
Minna's life gleams with muck, *Is it that reporter?*
Minna says that that might be it.
Elisabeth sighs.
Elisabeth reaches for her purse.
Minna knows what's coming: the prescription.
Elisabeth's into Ayurvedic medicine.
Ayurvedic medicine stems from India.
Ayurvedic medicine divides people into types.
Elisabeth is fire, Elisabeth says.
Minna's mud.
No one's surprised.

Elisabeth's been to the Bookstore of the Unknown.
Elisabeth's bought a book about demons.
The demons are Indian.
The book's dust jacket is black.
Elisabeth says that the book will provide Minna with fire.
Indian demons are good at rage.
Demons transform through destruction.
Minna watches her sister's face: it actually opens up.
The face is a soup pot of crazy ideas.
The sister feels certain the reporter can be exorcized.
Minna will see, it'll be a relief.
Minna looks at the book and understands.
Minna's a weak creature.
Elisabeth's stronger.
Minna thanks her.
Minna's a pleaser.
Elisabeth's rage is a legend in the family, but
Elisabeth's doing better now.
Elisabeth gets up and adjusts her clothing.
*A vacuum cleaner wouldn't hurt*, Elisabeth says.
Minna nods.
*Aarhus is still on the map*, Elisabeth says.
Minna nods.
*Dad got to be old as the hills.*
Minna nods.
*Life goes on.*
Minna nods.
*It's really late*, her sister says.
Minna nods and nods and nods.

*

Elisabeth's demons lie on the night table.
Minna can't sleep.
The demons sneak about in the dark.
The demons reek of soot.
Minna switches on the light and opens the door to the kitchen stairs.
Minna goes down into the backyard and its twilight.
The man in number eight's watching soccer.
The woman in number four's having sex.
The stars twinkle.
The trashcan gapes.
Minna casts the demons from her and closes the lid.
Minna opens the lid again.
Minna jams the book under a bag.
It's not enough.
Minna jams it farther down.
Minna can feel the trash around her hand.
Minna feels the trash's soft and hard parts.
Minna gets damp fingers.
Minna gets her upper arm in.
Minna thinks of vets and midwives.
Minna's as deep down as she can get.
Minna releases the book.
The book's wedged in there deep down.
Minna hauls up her damp arm.
Minna averts her face from the stench.
Minna presses the lid down hard.
The man in number eight scores.
The woman in number four ditto.
Minna goes back upstairs.

Minna scrubs herself.
Minna goes to bed.
Minna can't sleep.
You never know with demons.
Demons are parasites.
Parasites need individuals.
Minna knows that.
Minna's an individual herself.
Minna's one individual among millions.
Minna's a gnu on the savannah.
Minna's a herring in a barrel, but even worse:
Minna places her hands across her eyes.
Minna feels something: *Was that hair?*
Minna slips out to the mirror.
Minna places her face against it, and there she is:
Minna with fur on her face.
Minna in a wild stampede.
Minna on her way over the cliff edge.
The sea waiting below.
Death by drowning.
Her paws paddling and paddling.
The paws cannot, they cannot.
The orchestra plays a psalm.
Minna can no longer sing.
Minna sinks quietly toward the bottom.
Minna doesn't struggle at all.
Minna doesn't understand it herself.
Minna tells her mirror image, *Swim then, God damn it*, but Minna doesn't swim.

*

The sun's shining.
Jette's placed the paper across her knee.
The paper's opened to the culture section.
The front page of the culture section is full of a woman.
The woman is Linda Lund.
Minna balances two cups of coffee.
Jette's busy smoothing out the paper.
Minna's having a hard time getting her legs to bend.
Minna glances at the mermaid's gaping gaze.
Minna glances at Linda.
Linda fills most of the front page.
Linda's shot with an out-of-focus lens.
Linda's mouth is slightly open.
Linda's eyes are deep and alert.
Linda sits and strokes her guitar.
The guitar no longer plays Segovia.
The guitar plays wistful pop.
People love wistful pop.
The guitar's positioned between Linda's legs.
People love Linda's legs.
Minna has goblins in her diaphragm.
Minna turns green.
Minna's terrible to photograph.
Minna's better in person, but
Linda looks lovely in the paper.
Minna can't breathe.
Minna's throat stings.
Jette rustles the paper excessively.
Jette lifts it up.
The paper's right in Minna's face.

Minna sees what Jette wants to show her:
Lars has written the article.
Lars has made the article fill seven columns.
Lars has used the word *sensual* in the headline.
Minna looks toward Christianshavn.
Jette knocks back her coffee.
*Things are going well for Linda*, Jette says.
Minna's tongue feels cold as bronze.
Minna's body starts shutting down.
The face chilly.
The heart pounding.
The larynx a clenched fist.
Nothing comes out.
Jette asks, *How's Lars, really?*
Minna's fingers tighten around her coffee.
Jette asks, *Do you still see each other?*
Minna has sat down but can't remain sitting.
Minna gets up and hops around a bit.
Minna has to pee.
Minna has to go to the john twice a day on average when she's at the Royal Library.

*

Minna wants to tell someone about her broken heart.
Minna feels pain in the solar plexus of her soul.
Minna needs a hot-water bottle.
Finn answers the phone.
Finn wants to chat.
Finn's a birdwatcher.
Finn's seen a bittern.

Finn knows where the nightingale lives.
Minna asks for Mom.
Mom comes to the phone.
Mom's glad to hear from her.
Minna's just about to cry, but
Mom and Finn have been to the Skaw.
Mom and Finn saw someone famous in a car.
Mom and Finn took a hike on Grenen.
The wind was blowing sand.
*The sand got into everything.*
Mom says that she misses Minna.
Mom feels like it's been a long time.
The clump in Minna's throat gets bigger.
The clump's a doorstop.
Minna can't say anything.
Mom goes quiet on the other end.
Mom and Minna are quiet together.
Minna whispers that she'll definitely come visit.
*It won't be long*, Minna says.
Mom says that of course they could come to Copenhagen.
Time's one thing they've got plenty of.
Minna doesn't like that Mom says *they*.
Minna says they'd be very welcome.
*Minna says we should go to Copenhagen*, Mom says.
Finn's indistinct in the background.
Mom laughs.
Mom tells her about the geraniums.
The geraniums are thriving in the east-facing windows.
The geraniums have an acrid scent in the sun.
The geraniums get photographed.

The geraniums get posted on the web.
Minna should go in and see.
Minna promises to look at Mom's blog.
Minna keeps her promise.
Mom's blog is kept rose pink.
Mom's blog is mostly photos, but
Text sneaks its way in between the geraniums.
Mom's written about her daughters on the blog.
The daughters live far away in Copenhagen.
The elder one's married to an optician.
The younger is unwed.
Mom isn't a grandma.
*You can't get everything you wish for*, Mom writes.
Minna stares at the text.
The text is more intimate than Mom's Christmas letter to the family.
The text is more naked than Minna's seen Mom in real life.
*Nobody really reads it anyhow*, Mom must've thought.
*Somebody might read it by accident*, Mom must've thought.
Both thoughts had appealed.
It started small.
It began as a lift of the skirt.
It took root gradually.
The web's become a diary for Mom.
Mom starts to versify.
Mom writes haiku.
Mom lets it all hang out.
The geraniums are pink and demure, but
Mom's stark naked.
Minna hastens to shut it off.

Minna considers calling up the Senior Club.
The Senior Club ought to explain the gravity to seniors.
The web's a jungle.
The jungle's full of monkeys.
Monkeys love the excrement of others.

*

Lars has had Linda on the front page.
Elisabeth's been in the Bookstore of the Unknown.
Jette sits on the quay.
Mom's on the web too often.
Dad's dead.
Lars has fur on his face, but
Lars's fur isn't quite like Minna's.
Minna's fur is a metaphor.
Lars's fur is real.
Minna's studied portraits.
Lars and Dad have a beard in common, but
Lars smelled of Aqua Velva.
Dad of salt.
Minna's looked at the map of Denmark.
Aarhus nestles in Marselisborg Forest.
Amager's on the other end of the country, or
Amager's in the middle of the country, or
Amager's in any case quiet for a brief moment.
The quiet makes room.
The quiet makes a dome over a moment's clarity.
The clarity lays bare a person.
The person is Minna herself.
Minna hasn't seen her own person for a long time.

Minna's person has split ends.
Minna's person has bags.
The person's hand trembles quietly.
The person's mouth hangs open.
Minna can hear a faint hum.
Minna thinks, *I used to sing . . .*
Minna gives herself the once-over.
Minna benefits from the examination.
Time now for a little holiday.
Other people aren't to join the holiday.
Minna hasn't been to Bornholm since she was fourteen.
Bornholm's almost Sweden.
Bornholm's in the opposite direction.
Bornholm's an island.
Bornholm's well suited to mental catharsis.
Lars will be forgotten.
The family'll have to take care of itself.
The family *can* take care of itself.
Minna orders a ticket to Ystad.
Minna wants to develop an ability to sort people out.
Minna wants an asshole filter.
Minna no longer wants to be a host species.
Minna takes Bergman along.
Bergman can ride in the backpack.

*

Minna's sitting on the train to Ystad.
Minna's feeling chipper.
Minna's running away from it all.
Minna's breaking from the pack.

The pack is evil.
Minna doesn't want to be part of them.
Minna's wistful too.
Minna was sure one grew out of it.
Minna thought as a kid, *As soon as I grow up*, but
Grown-ups are kids who have lots to hide.
Dumb kids become dumb grown-ups.
Evil kids = evil grown-ups.
Minna gets the connection.
Minna walks around among ordinary people.
Ordinary people cheat on their taxes.
Ordinary people visit swinger clubs.
Ordinary people flee the scene of the crime.
Ordinary people enlist in the Nordland Regiment of the SS.
Ordinary people are quislings, collaborators, camp followers.
Ordinary people just need a stage.
The pig performs gladly.
Cowards are also in good supply.
Minna doesn't get how she could have looked past it.
Minna's clear-sighted enough.
Minna's watched TV.
Minna followed the war in the Balkans.
Minna watched neighbors outing each other to Serbian militias.
One day you're tending cabbage together in the backyard.
The next you're on a bus headed for a mass grave.
Your best friend's a chameleon.
Evil's a state that can be conjured.
Evil exists.
Minna supposes she's tarred with the same brush.
Karin's not exactly without stain either.

Elisabeth is family.
Lars could've been.
Minna realizes that it's all about sorting.
Minna's got to judge people one at a time.
Minna wants to learn not to trust.
That'll all be over now.
The last narcissist's gotten her to clap.
The last Jutlander's taken up residence in her inbox.
The last nymphomaniac.
The last reporter.
Indian demons.
Billy goats.
Kamikaze pilots.
Thieves in the night:
It's over!
Minna feels her backbone grow.
Minna's backbone sends out roots and shoots.
Minna's backbone blossoms.
Minna looks out upon the southern Swedish landscape.
The landscape drifts past like a fog.
*Grown-ups are kids who become like animals*, Minna thinks.
Minna tries dozing.
The train's got a school camp on board.
The school camp's blocked all exits.
The teacher screams that the school camp has to settle down a bit.
The teacher screams, *SO SIT DOWN, FREDERIK!*
The teacher screams, *THERE ARE OTHER PEOPLE ON THE TRAIN!*
*That might be so*, Minna thinks, but
Bergman's the only human on the train.
Bergman lies on her lap.

*Dread makes the dreaded real.*
That's true – or . . .
Minna listens to the school camp.
Minna dreaded *not* having a kid.
The school camp relieves the fear.
Kids are sweet, but
Kids reflect their parents' seamy side.
Bergman knows that.
Bergman had nine kids.
Bergman had to make films to get away from his kids.
Minna shouldn't be down in the mouth.
Anne Marie Carl-Nielsen's also along on the trip.
Anne Marie's along in Minna's mind.
Anne Marie preferred animals.
Anne Marie was into mermaids and horses.
Minna's more into cats, but
Minna will make do alone.
Minna's a composer!
Minna settles into her seat, thrilled about the ferry.
The Baltic is capricious.
The Baltic's deep and smooth.
The Baltic's a bowl, a submarine valley.
The Baltic's as balmy as a bathtub.
Minna's brought her bathing suit along.
It's late in August.
Minna's stoked.
Minna's heading away from what hurts.
*No one's going to inflict any more damage*, Minna thinks.
*Everything's going to get sorted*, Minna thinks, because
Minna wants to grow an asshole filter.

Minna thinks she can grow it quickly.
Minna's broken heart dwells in the breast of an optimist.

*

Minna's boarded the *Leonora Christine*.
The school camp's shepherded onto the upper deck.
The school camp's met another school camp.
The school camps exchange sexual fluids.
Minna drinks coffee in the stern canteen.
The canteen's full of retirees.
The retirees swarm up from the vehicle deck.
The retirees want to sit with one other.
Minna moves gladly.
Minna moves for two pairs of friends in their mid-seventies.
The gentlemen immediately order beer.
The missuses have newly permed hair.
The missuses make do with orange soda.
The gentlemen squeeze their permed missuses.
The missuses giggle.
The retirees have sex.
Minna can see that they have sex.
Minna thinks of Mom.
Minna dismisses the thought.
The thought lands on Lars.
Lars without clothes on.
Lars with a hard-on.
Minna on horseback.
Cat on a hot tin roof.
Minna and Lars, genital to genital, no respect.
Minna blushes on the plastic ferry seat.

Minna's been the fuck buddy of a disrespectful man.
*That's the way it is*, thinks Minna.
Minna's backbone withers.
Lars prefers sex with a machete.
It's unbearable, but there you have it.
The retirees raise their glasses.
Minna takes up Bergman from her pack.
The *Leonora Christine* pulls away from the quay.
The *Leonora Christine* heads out.
Minna glances down at Bergman.
Bergman says, *I pretend to be an adult.*
Bergman says, *Time and again it amazes me that people take me seriously.*
Minna loves Bergman.
Bergman lunges for Minna with the truth.
Bergman holds her tight, and now she glances at the door to the vehicle deck.
The door opens.
A small group of retirees trickles in.
Minna feels initially serene at the sight.
It doesn't last.
Minna raises Bergman to her face.
Minna slouches in her seat.
Minna wants to get off the *Leonora Christine*.
The *Leonora Christine* has set course for Rønne, but
Minna wants to leave.
Minna was once a music teacher at a folk high school.
Minna taught weeklong classes for happy amateurs.
The happy amateurs signed up in torrents.
The folk high school provided housing.

The folk high school was always going bust.
The amateurs had dough.
People stood there with guitars and piccolos.
People wanted to be virtuous.
Minna tried to teach them a bit of notation.
Minna clapped in time.
Minna played Bach for them.
Minna was trampled by dwarfs.
Minna ran out of options.
Minna let them sing from the tired Danish songbook.
The amateurs sang, *Is the light only for the learnèd?*
Minna had her own take.
The amateurs felt disgruntled about their rooms.
Minna found them new ones.
The amateurs lost their things:
Dentures, rollators, and spectacles vanishing every instant.
Prosthetic legs and large-print books: gone.
Grundtvig hovered above the waters.
Grundtvig illuminated the scene.
Grundtvig was high on sugar water and the life of
the mind.
Minna had to see to all the practicalities herself.
The amateurs loved Minna.
The amateurs pinched her on the cheek.
The amateurs wanted to sing at the farewell party.
The party was full of music that Minna had inflicted on
their world.
Minna wept.
Minna felt ashamed.
Minna needed rent.

Minna was keeping the wolf from the door, but
The wolf was preferable in the end.
Minna quit and is now en route to Bornholm.
Minna sits behind Bergman on the *Leonora Christine*.
Minna has recognized the hindmost retiree.
The retiree's named Gunvor Kramer.
Gunvor Kramer's a happy amateur.
Gunvor Kramer's a sincere person, but even worse:
Gunvor's on Facebook, and even worse:
Gunvor's convinced that she and Minna are colleagues.
Gunvor recorded a Christmas tape.
Gunvor recorded it on a reel-to-reel.
The reel-to-reel stands in Gunvor's living room.
Gunvor is thus a composer.
Gunvor writes Minna often.
Gunvor writes about her breakthroughs in the art of music,
but even worse:
Gunvor Kramer's aboard the *Leonora Christine*.
Gunvor Kramer's set a course for Minna.
Minna knows that her holiday hangs by a thread.
Gunvor's in a car, you see.
Gunvor would like to chauffeur Minna around the island.
Gunvor would like to sing all her compositions for Minna,
vibrato.
Minna presses Bergman to her face.
Gunvor passes by somewhere to the rear.
Gunvor walks slowly, slowly.
Minna turns cautiously.
Gunvor has sat down two booths away, with her back
to Minna.

It's silly of course.
Gunvor's merely a person.
Gunvor loves #544 in the tired Danish songbook.
Gunvor loves chain dancing.
Gunvor has a droopy bosom.
Minna was dragged in as an unwilling witness.
Minna tucks Bergman into her backpack.
Minna rediscovers her sunglasses.
The sunglasses slip down in front of her face.
Gunvor's started on the candy catalogue.
Gunvor's found a ballpoint pen.
Gunvor sets checkmarks by candy.
The sunglasses shield Minna from Gunvor.
Minna passes Gunvor.
Minna's set a course for the stern.
Minna catches sight of the sea.
The Baltic lies blue and piercing.
The *Leonora Christine* shoves its way forward, self-confidence in its hull.
The *Leonora Christine* heads down the coast.
Minna slouches in a seat.
Minna hugs her backpack.
Minna oozes adrenaline.
Swedish customs opens for candy and liquor purchasers.
Swedish customs is full of retirees.
Gunvor forages.
Minna leans back.
No one heeds her anymore.
Minna's alone and can plan her escape.

*

Minna's arrived in Rønne.
Elisabeth's gotten a hold of her.
Mom's making plans for the weekend, but
Minna isn't home.
Elisabeth wants to know where she is, but
Minna's just not home.
Bornholm waits in the sunshine.
Bus #5 swoops across the island.
Minna's looking forward to seeing the landscape again.
Minna's quickly disappointed.
Bornholm had more cliffs in her memory.
Bornholm was exotic, Swedish.
Bornholm seems abandoned now.
The bus stop spots are dusty.
The butcher's closed.
The baker, the dairy, the school.
Bjarne's tanning salon has set up shop in the supermarket.
Bjarne's tanning salon browns the serfs.
Bjarne's tanning salon turns little girls into reality stars.
Bjarne makes a mint on the villages' decline.
The province assuages grief with porn.
The houses are cheap.
The houses have signs in their windows.
The houses are OPEN, OPEN, OPEN.
Most folks have fled.
Randiness remains.
Minna can see that a country is about to disappear.
Minna can see that the tracks point over the cliff edge.
Minna feels like a slum tourist.
*That wasn't the idea with this holiday*, thinks Minna.

Minna regards a shelter in Østerlars.
The round church has wandered off.
The round church has taken a room in Copenhagen.
Grief is latent in Minna.
Grief seizes its chance.
Minna gets moisture in her eyes.
Minna wipes the moisture away.
Minna wants to find a rock in the sea.
Minna wants to go out to the rock and sit.
Bergman will join her, and a thermos of coffee.
The cliffs begin someplace.
Minna googled Svaneke.
Minna saw the cliffs on the web.
The idyll will take over sooner or later.
Minna glances down in her backpack.
The cellphone sits down there.
Elisabeth's name throbs like an irate artery.
Minna shuts the pack.
Minna can see a large field of grain.
Minna can see a steep slope.
Bus #5 drives through the grain.
The sea appears at the foot of the hill.
The Baltic doubles over, vast and wet.
Bus #5 is headed toward Listed, and now it happens.
Bornholm opens up.
Bornholm looks like itself in the pictures.
The smokehouse has a flame under the herring.
Troll figurines have appeared in the windows.
The cliffs fall crumbling into the water.
The sea is blue-black, with swans in it.

The bus winds through charming houses.
The bus holds for a school camp.
The bus holds for another school camp.
The bus holds for a flock of retirees.
The bus swings gently down the coast and into Svaneke.
Minna presses the STOP button.
The bus stops by the hard-candy store.
Minna struggles with her wheeled suitcase, and then she's standing there.
Minna stands there and is reminded of the Old Town in Aarhus.
Minna's reminded of the trips to Ballehage Beach.
Minna remembers her toes on the pier.
Minna with webbed feet.
Minna with piano fingers.
Minna with song in her throat.
Minna with a future before her, but
Elisabeth rings loudly in the pack.
Elisabeth's on Minna's trail.
Minna refuses to yield.
Minna fumbles in her pocket for the address.
Minna's going to live in a room with a tea kitchen.
The room has a view across the harbor.
The landlady's a friend of a friend.
Minna's not hoping that the landlady's gregarious.
Minna wants to be alone in the Baltic.
Minna stands quietly on the square.
Minna sees people everywhere.
The people are speaking Copenhagen dialect.
The people are looking for a ceramist.
Minna stands in the people's way.

Minna must make way.
Minna wheels her suitcase forward and back.
Minna's in the midst of a transport tsunami.

*

The lodgings in this case are not lacking.
Half-timbering goes with everything.
The foundation is Bornholm granite.
The room has a table, sofa, and bed.
The room isn't missing a thing, *au contraire*.
The room has latticed windows with geraniums.
Minna's rubbed the scented leaves between her fingers.
Minna's said hello to the landlady.
The landlady was in her mid-forties.
The landlady bore the mark of tourism.
Minna said that she had to quote *work during her stay*.
Minna's used that trick before.
People with projects are left in peace.
Minna has the one end of the house.
The door between Minna and the landlady is locked.
*Nobody'll come barging in*, the landlady promised.
That's great, and yet it isn't anyway.
The landlady's got a dog.
The dog bays.
The dog's bayed ever since the landlady left to do her shopping.
Minna sees the dog before her:
The dog's muzzle pointed skyward.
The dog's lower lip pushed forward.
The dog's eyes squinting ceilingward.

The dog doesn't want to be alone.
Minna's just the other side of the landlady's locked door.
The dog can hear Minna.
The dog doesn't understand that Minna can't rescue it.
Minna's hushed the dog through the keyhole.
Minna's acted as if she's gone to the grocery store.
The dog isn't fooled by cheap tricks.
The dog has nothing to do but complain about the program.
Minna puts her earplugs into action.
Minna sits in a soundproof bubble.
Minna can hear her breathing in the bubble.
Minna's lungs puff quietly.
Minna's pulse vibrates.
Minna closes her eyes and listens.
The ocean buzzes in Minna's veins.
The ocean calls from Minna's interior.
The ocean's outside the window, but
The ocean's inside Minna too.
Minna sits with the sea inside.
Minna ought to go for a walk, she knows.
Svaneke awaits outside and lovely.
People circle like good-natured sharks.
Minna should walk past them and out to a cliff, but
Minna's deaf and listens.
Minna's interior is a rehash of memories.
Minna paddles around in the old days.
Minna feels her body shifting.
Minna's senses are returning.
Hands down through the sand.
Hands up toward the gulls.

Dad's hand and Minna's.
The blue delta of Dad's hand.
The sea rises in Minna.
The sea finds fissures in Minna.
Minna's leaky.
Minna opens her eyes and blinks.
The sea trickles slowly.
The sea reaches land.
The beads of gravel rattle.
Minna blows her nose.
Minna should find herself a cliff.
Minna and Bergman should walk out onto the cliff and sit.
Minna shouldn't do anything else.
Minna thinks that Gunvor's peeping in the window.
The geraniums block the inward view.
Bornholm's relatively large.
The likelihood's small, but
Minna peeks out from behind a plant.
Svaneke harbor rocks with boats.
The tourists balance glass plates.
The tourists turn the corner in sensible shoes.
The tourists position themselves willingly in line.
The cliffs are out there.
The cliffs are warm from the day's sun.
Minna runs a hand across her face.
Minna opens her backpack.
Bergman's lying down there.
*Dread makes the dreaded real*, he repeats.
Minna nods.
Minna closes her eyes.

Minna whispers out into the lodgings: *Now the dog howls no more.*
*The dog's done with playing forsaken.*
*The dog's shut its mouth.*
*The dog lies in its basket.*
*The dog begs for its ball.*
*The dog has nothing more to say about its situation.*
Minna removes the earplug on the right side.
Minna listens with her head cocked.
—
The dog howls.
The dog howls skyward.

*

Minna's crawled out as far as she can go.
Minna sits on the blanket she brought.
The granite drills up gently into her buttock.
The gulls have set up camp on a couple cliffs farther out.
Christiansø is a seed on the horizon.
Christiansø beckons with its outpost nature.
Minna doesn't want to be any farther out now.
Minna just wants to sit here.
Minna wants to drink her coffee with Bergman.
The waves smack gently against the cliff.
The world smells of seaweed.
Minna sits and is doing fine.
Minna comes to think of Vagn.
Minna took a first-aid course of Vagn's.
Minna's never rescued anyone, but
Vagn knew all about hurt people.

Vagn said, *Hold their hand!*
Vagn said, *Bodily contact helps the injured!*
Vagn said, *Caresses and calm speech'll pass the time.*
*The ambulance'll get there sooner or later.*
*A human being could use another human in the meantime.*
*A small hand is enough!*
Minna looks around her circle of acquaintances.
The circle of acquaintances can't get a hand out through the shield.
The circle of acquaintances can't get skin on skin.
Minna considers her hand.
Minna doesn't need to play pious.
Minna's hand has withdrawn from the struggle.
Minna's hand hasn't touched anyone since Lars.
Lars was so real under the duvet.
Lars was so gentle down there.
Lars dared in the dark, but
The light demands trend awareness.
Minna's not trendy.
Minna's soft and warm every day.
The everyday doesn't cut it.
Minna takes her hand from the sea and sticks it in her mouth.
The sea tastes good.
The lighthouse towers behind her.
Årsdale nestles to the south.
Christiansø is Denmark's remotest enclave.
*This rock's a rehearsal space*, thinks Minna.
The gulls are the only ones present.
Minna can make noise the way she wishes.
Minna feels something slipping far below.

Minna's belly grows in capacity.
The lungs become bellows.
The throat a swan's.
The voice full of rust.
Minna's needed rehearsal space, but
Bornholm's big.
Bornholm has no objection if Minna warbles a trill.
*The song has light*, Minna sings.
Minna doesn't know where it's coming from, but it persists.
*The song has warmth*, she sings.
Minna recalls the folk high school now.
*The song has eternity.*
Minna thinks it's a strange song.
Minna sings the song anyway.
Minna's voice rises plumb upward.
The voice is like a beanpole.
Minna can climb it.
Minna can reach the stars.
Minna can reach the giant, the golden eggs, the empyrean.
Minna's good at climbing, but then she dives.
It does the voice good to plunge headlong.
The voice breaks the surface of the sea.
The voice continues toward the bottom.
The sea grass sways and tickles.
The marine fauna stands still and listens.
The voice is alone with itself and the wet.
Minna closes her eyes and she sings,
*The song unites as it fades.*
That's not enough for Minna.
Minna gives the song a last burst.

Minna's heart lifts.
The gulls rise.
The wings flutter.
The wings applaud and applaud.
Minna opens her eyes, and there stands an angler.
The angler stands on the rock ten yards away.
The angler looks at Minna.
The angler creaks in his rubber boots.
The angler calls out,
*The fish are getting spooked.*
Minna blushes: *I thought I was alone.*
A kayaker instantly paddles past.
Another kayaker, and yet another.
The kayakers paddle past like geese in a village pond.
The angler points somewhere behind Minna.
Minna turns around.
The evening sun is blinding, but there sit a man and a woman.
The man and woman wave with their cigarettes.
The woman says that it sounded lovely.
Minna repeats that she thought she was alone.
The woman and the man often sit by the lighthouse in the evening.
*The view of Christiansø*, says the man.
*The view of the bathers*, says the woman.
The woman points at a springboard a little ways off.
People are leaping from the springboard down among the cliffs.
The campground tents sprout up among the brush.
Minna doesn't want to know anything else, but
The couple's from Østerbro in Copenhagen.
The couple could stay on Bornholm forever.

The woman pinches the man on the thigh.
The man pinches the woman on the thigh.
The man has large lips.
The woman isn't wearing a bra.
Minna wishes it weren't embarrassing to leave.
Bergman smiles at her from down on the granite.
Bergman declares that she's never been lovelier, but
Bergman would lie worse than a horse runs if his prick were in a pickle.
*Flight is a sign of weakness*, she whispers.
Silence descends.
Silence is no longer a balm for the soul.
Silence is a social defect.
Minna feels the need to converse a bit.
Minna asks whether the couple has a cottage.
The woman says the cottage belongs to her husband.
The husband in question isn't along on holiday.
The man with the large lips on the other hand is along for the whole trip.
The man asks Minna where she's from.
Minna doesn't know what to say.
Minna has more of an impulse to cry.
*Aarhus—*, says Minna.
Minna is suddenly unsure.
Minna felt at home in the song a few minutes ago.
The song disappeared, down toward the bottom.
The song stands still among the herring.
Everything else belongs to another reality.
*Everything else*, Minna thinks to herself, *is mere geography.*

*

Minna's crawled into bed at her lodgings.
The landlady's not home.
The dog's inconsolable.
Minna's stuffed a quilt around the bottom of the door.
Minna's glad she has earplugs.
Minna's glad she's by herself again.
The man and woman wanted to accompany her to Svaneke.
Minna was dragged in as an unwilling witness.
Minna didn't escape the couple till they were at the harbor kiosk.
Disappointment inhabits her mind like rainy weather.
Minna really wants an asshole filter.
Minna wants to start setting limits.
Minna can't say yes or no, and
Minna's legs feel heavy.
The duvet feels strange.
The lodgings smell of cottage.
Minna thinks of spooks.
Minna's only afraid of spooks once in a while.
Minna doesn't believe in spooks, but
Things you don't believe in often exist anyway.
The Grauballe Man haunted Minna one spring when she was a child.
The Grauballe Man lay dead in the Moesgaard Museum, but
The Grauballe Man walks around at night.
The Grauballe Man wriggles out of his display.
The Grauballe Man stands out on the cobblestones.
The Grauballe Man walks into Marselisborg Forest.
The Grauballe Man loves nature – and Minna.
The bog man in any case visits Minna at night.

Minna lies in her small bed with the duvet pulled up to her nose.
Minna lies and stares at the door of her room.
The living room resounds with the sound of coffee cups.
Elisabeth's room resounds with the sound of high-school boys.
Minna lies with her eyes on stalks, and then!
The door opens, and who should enter?
Minna's friend from Marselisborg Forest.
The Grauballe Man smells of harness.
The Grauballe Man's body is a story of its own.
The head crushed.
The throat cut.
The feet flat and lumpy, but what's worse:
The bog man leans over Minna.
The bog man's picked anemones for Minna.
The bog man boasts of his earthly remains.
The bog man still has flesh on his bones.
Minna will end up a skeleton!
Dad too!
Mom!
Elisabeth?
Minna doesn't believe in spooks.
Minna believes in the Grauballe Man.
Minna lies in her Bornholm sanctuary.
Minna considers the spiritual probabilities.
Bergman haunts her too.
Elisabeth employs demons.
The Fenris wolf howls.
The spooks are coming if they exist.
Elisabeth's coming if she discovers where Minna is.
Elisabeth wants to have the little ones under her thumb.

Minna just wants to love the little ones.
Minna's little ones would never lack for sweets.
Minna's little ones would grow roly-poly.
Minna really can't say no.
It doesn't matter now anyhow.
Minna won't become anyone's mother, and
Kids are the worst spooks in the world.
Kids can't understand that they don't exist.
Kids stick their cold hands under the duvet.
Kids would like to slap the sleeper's face.
Minna collects herself.
Minna forces herself to think of dull things.
Minna makes plans for the morrow.
Minna wants to go farther out.
Minna wants to find a rock so desolate.
Minna wants to go out to the rock and sing.
Minna wants to make sure she's alone.
Minna wants to stand there and get everything to swing.
The song will vault higher and higher.
The sky will stretch itself open,
The waves cast themselves against the cliff,
The ships beat into the wind.
Minna presses herself down into her rented linen.
Minna pushes herself out of reality.
The children exit Minna's consciousness.
The children go with the Grauballe Man.
Marselisborg Forest closes up after them.
The museum awaits.
The roe deer.

*

Minna's put on her bathing suit under her sundress.
Minna wants to go out and sing and get a tan.
Minna wants to rock-bathe.
Minna has to get provisions first.
Minna's gone for a walk in town.
Svaneke's lovely.
Svaneke's light yellow.
*Svaneke's a set piece*, thinks Minna.
The sky a stage border.
The smokehouse a sort of canteen.
The knickknack shops = the costume department.
Minna plays with the motif, and there's something to it.
Minna does like Svaneke, but
Svaneke reminds her a bit of Linda.
The houses have tricked themselves out for the season.
The houses bulge with whitewashed plinths.
Minna raises her eyes to the horizon.
The ocean's not going anywhere.
The ocean's seen much worse.
The cliffs are above thoughts of time.
The Baltic, Årsdale!
Minna wants to hike toward Årsdale a bit later.
Minna wants to hike so far south that she can hike in peace.
Minna's looked at the map.
The rocks extend a long way out down there.
The rocks permit clambering.
Minna can walk far out onto the rocks.
Minna's on her way down and out, but
Svaneke Dairy is famed for its beer ice cream.
Svaneke Dairy lies en route.

Minna wants to have an ice cream to hike on.
The weather's good for ice cream, and lots of people have thought the same thing:
The tourists have formed a line.
The line reaches far out into the gravel.
The line hardly budges.
The small children crawl around on a plastic cow in the courtyard.
The mothers stand in line.
The fathers look after the kids.
The retirees rummage in their purses.
The retirees cannot find their spectacles.
The waitresses are dressed in Morten Korch costumes.
The waitresses resemble actresses from the Fifties.
The waitresses look like Tove Maës and Ghita Nørby.
The waitresses hobble becomingly in their feudal shoes.
The waitresses look homespun by the latte machines.
Minna's crept forward a little ways in the line now.
Minna can see that there are celebrities in the line.
The celebrities take a long time to serve.
The retirees are on a first-name basis with the celebrities.
The small children ride the cow.
The fathers look at smartphones.
The mothers are ready to crack.
Minna on the other hand is of good cheer.
Minna wants to have a cup of coffee with her ice cream.
Minna's advanced far in the line.
Minna's about to order.
Tove Maës just can't see Minna.
Tove Maës can only see the celebrity.

The celebrity's from on TV.
The celebrity will have ice cream with licorice in it.
The celebrity will have espresso.
The celebrity flaunts the fact that he comes here often.
Tove Maës and the celebrity gossip about the locals.
Ghita Nørby limps out for more sherbet.
Ghita and Tove want to serve the celebrity best.
The celebrity can get what he wants.
Minna's been cut in front of twice now.
Minna raises her hand tentatively.
Minna gets up on tiptoe.
The celebrity laughs loud and long.
Tove Maës laughs loud and long.
The retirees' hip cement begins to crumble.
The kids will be confirmed soon.
The mothers and fathers have long since been divorced.
Minna says, *Excuse me!*
Minna's surprised to hear her own voice.
Minna continues, *There are lots of folks who're waiting.*
Tove Maës freezes under her bonnet.
Ghita Nørby moves in frames.
Minna blushes with justice on her side.
Minna orders a caffe latte.
Minna orders a tub of beer ice cream.
Tove Maës hobbles over to the coffee machine.
Ghita Nørby shoots the celebrity a glance.
The celebrity walks out into the courtyard.
The retiree behind Minna smiles gratefully.
Minna looks proudly back at the line.
Minna regards the people she's rescued.

Minna's proud of her sudden asshole filter.
Minna sticks a feather in her cap.
*Small victories count too*, she thinks.
A hand pokes up in the middle of the line.
The hand pokes up and waves.
A large gray head pops to the side.
Gunvor's mouth is a gaping O.
Gunvor calls out Minna's name loudly in the dairy.
*Minna! It's me! Gunvor Kramer! From the folk high school!*
Minna hears her coffee fizz out of the coffee machine.
Tove Maës sends a wicked smile out of the corner of her mouth.
Minna's asshole filter worked well two seconds ago, but
Minna's asshole filter has large holes in the mesh.

*

Gunvor Kramer's found a corner in the courtyard.
Gunvor Kramer's pushed Minna deep into the corner.
Gunvor Kramer's wearing a linen smock.
Gunvor Kramer's hair is pinned fast with a Viking clasp.
Gunvor's been thinking a lot about Minna.
Minna's made a big difference for Gunvor.
Gunvor was only capable of simple compositions.
Gunvor couldn't get larger works to hang together.
Gunvor mostly preferred music with a chorus.
Gunvor was stuck artistically.
Minna helped her advance.
Gunvor stands in the supermarket, and then it happens.
Gunvor has to run out of the store.
Gunvor has to go over to her car.
Gunvor seats herself behind the wheel.

Gunvor finds her notebook in her purse.
Gunvor writes down the lyrics.
Gunvor hums the melody.
*This is just an example*, says Gunvor.
Gunvor clears her throat.
Minna's coffee halts in front of her mouth.
The coffee steams in the morning heat.
The beer ice cream melts.
Gunvor sings a song.
The song's about love.
*Love is vulnerable*, sings Gunvor.
*Love falls to pieces so easy*, she sings.
*People are so busy.*
*No one should forget anyone.*
*No one should forget anyone.*
Gunvor's eyes are large and shiny.
Gunvor's finished now.
Gunvor says that it's the prologue to a cantata.
The cantata's still missing a lot.
Minna smiles and grasps her beer ice cream.
Minna moves over on the bench.
Minna says, *It's nice to know you got something out of the class.*
Gunvor scrapes the bottom of her sherbet tub.
Gunvor asks how long Minna's going to be on Bornholm.
Minna answers vaguely.
Gunvor gets an idea.
Gunvor's planned a day trip to Dueodde.
*It's hot*, Gunvor says, *let's go down and bathe.*
Minna says, *I'm not big on swimming.*
Gunvor points at her sundress and asks, *Why the bathing suit?*

Minna needn't reply.
Minna doesn't owe Gunvor a reply.
Gunvor's already moved on anyhow.
Gunvor tells her about the sand in Dueodde.
The sand is fine.
The sand gets into every fold of skin.
Gunvor slaps her thighs.
The skinfolds quiver.
Something moves inside the linen smock.
Minna feels powerless, especially in her face.
Minna needs to put up a fight.
Minna's mouth tries to come up with a lie.
Minna's mouth doesn't want to say anything.
Gunvor's mouth doesn't want anything but, but now Minna gets lucky:
The backpack rings.
Minna's backpack is sitting on the bench and ringing.
Gunvor looks at the backpack.
Minna knows quite well who's hiding in the pack.
Minna opens it up anyway.
People ought to go away when they talk on their cells.
Anything else is rude.
Minna presses the answer button.
Minna gets up carefully from the bench.
Minna leaves the corner with Gunvor.
*Minna here.*
*It's about time!* says Elisabeth.
Elisabeth gets down to business.
Elisabeth's been saving up.
Minna walks hesitantly through the courtyard.

Minna approaches the cow.
Elisabeth pricks up her ears on the other end.
Elisabeth asks, *Who are those kids?*
Minna says, *I don't know.*
That's true enough, but not true enough for the sister.
Elisabeth says that it's hard to be related to Minna.
Elisabeth says that it's getting harder and harder.
Elisabeth says that Mom and Finn are coming for the weekend.
Mom and Finn can't stay in Potato Row.
*The bench isn't for sitting on*, she says.
Elisabeth says that if Minna went to Aarhus more often.
Elisabeth says that it'd never happen if . . .
Minna's rounded the corner of the dairy.
Svaneke harbor lies before her.
The boats rock in the late summer breeze.
Gunvor sits in the courtyard.
Minna has her backpack with her.
Minna's sandals have non-slip soles.
Nothing's to prevent her.
The path is clear.
Who's going to stop her?
The sister wants to know where Minna is, and
Minna's running.
Minna's running down to the harbor.
Minna's on her way south, away from Svaneke.
Elisabeth says, *Answer me! Where?*
Minna says, *I'm on my way to Årsdale.*
Elisabeth doesn't know where Årsdale is.
*Årsdale's in North Jutland*, Minna says.
*Årsdale's a little place south of Aalborg.*

*Everyone knows that*, Minna says.
Minna can hear that Elisabeth didn't know that.
Minna can hear her sister's disbelief, but
Minna's positive, and now the connection's breaking up.
The connection crackles and hisses.
The connection gets so bad that Minna disappears.
Minna disappears.
Minna's feet take wing.
Minna's an instance of female buoyancy and helium.

*

The rock's flat and sloping.
The rock's wet at the base.
The sun hangs heavy as a plum.
The sea's blue-black.
Minna's seen it:
The Bay of Aarhus is a fresh blue plain.
The Sound's a bottle-green river, but
The Baltic's black and greasy.
Minna's taken off her sundress.
Minna's smeared herself with SPF 20.
Minna stands with her toes so that they get wet.
Minna wants to rock-bathe, but
The sea grass waves under the surface.
The bladderwrack has lashed itself fast.
The rock looks like a woman's sex under the surface.
Minna isn't really sure and glances behind her.
Minna had to clamber to get here.
Minna had to crawl and injure herself.
Minna had to rest en route.

Minna was in flight of course, but
Minna isn't thinking about Gunvor anymore.
Minna stares at the sea.
Minna sees the darkness shift downwards.
The darkness is deep on deep.
The loneliness profound.
Minna's got plenty of time.
Minna doesn't have to throw herself in.
The sky's vaulting.
The clouds assume their positions.
Minna's belly swells.
Something trickles.
Something else slides.
Minna lays her hands upon her midriff.
Minna inhales deep into her lungs.
Minna tilts back her neck.
Minna makes her mouth round, and then it arrives:
Minna sings a song in Latin.
Minna sings it with all that should've been.
Minna doesn't pull her punches:
*Sed eligo quod video*
*Collum iugo prebeo;*
*Ad iugum tamen*
*Suave suave transeo.*
The song feels like an incantation.
Latin has a menacing effect.
The words are like holy water.
The pelvis swaying.
The arms floating.
The feet stomping.

Minna chanting.
The sea licking her toes.
The song begins anew.
The song presses its way out again and again.
Minna senses the water's presence at her feet.
Minna thinks it's just grand getting cold feet.
Minna raises her voice as loud as it'll go.
The voice'll go very loud.
The voice can go maybe just loud enough too.
Minna wants to take a step backward.
The rock is slippery.
Minna's foot slips.
Minna slips with it.
Minna's legs rail against the sky.
Minna's head plunges toward stone.
Minna lands badly on her skull.
The skull breaks the fall of an entire woman.
Minna slides down into the water.
Minna slides down through the seaweed.
Minna sinks like a stone.
Minna's arms plow the water.
Minna's eyes are open and alive.
Minna's mouth is moist and round.
The sea feels like sweet chill.
The Baltic is a bowl.
The Baltic's a submarine valley.
Beauty won't deny itself.
The fish scoot off in gleaming procession.
The fish turn and pivot for Minna.
The scales glitter.

The eyes shine silver.
Minna reverts downward.
Minna wriggles her arms.
Minna waves to the darkness.
The darkness waves back.
Minna sees a gestalt in the darkness.
The gestalt has a beard.
The gestalt's mouth is a soft wet brushstroke.
Chest hair forces its way upward.
The beard wanders downward away from its chin.
An Adam's apple lies in the middle of the hair.
*Dad?* Minna thinks.
Dad waves.
Dad takes hold of Minna.
The fauna closes around them.
Bubbles seep from nose and mouth.
Hair flutters like sea grass.
Minna's pelvis has never been so round.
Minna's legs fuse and articulate.
Dad smiles at Minna.
Dad swims around Minna.
Minna says, *Helgenæs?*
Minna gets water in her mouth.
Minna gets a lot of water in her mouth.
Minna's lungs squeeze.
The lungs stretch.
The lungs are hard as cement.
The lungs don't want anything but to go upward.
Minna could happily continue downward, but
Minna's lungs want to go up.

Minna's bruised skull like a cork.
Minna's skull directional.
Minna's arms wretched fins.
Minna's legs kick and thrash.
The legs strike bedrock.
Minna's hands strike granite.
The rocks close around Minna.
Minna grasps the seaweed strands.
Minna grabs hold of Bornholm from below.
Minna throws up her arms in late-summerness.
Minna scrabbles on stone.
Minna searches for a chink.
Minna contracts like a muscle before it explodes.
Minna clings to dry land, angry and insecure.
Minna's tongue feels cold as bronze.
The sun acting up.
The corneas drying out.
Minna hauls herself farther up, and then she lies there.
Minna has rock-bathed.
Minna's been down and out.
Minna's toes plash in the surface of the ocean.
The rest of Minna has been decently salvaged.
Minna's world stands still.
Minna thinks of Dad in the water.
Minna thinks of her head.
Minna's head was apparently injured a bit.
The head hurting.
The mouth spitting.
Snot running.
The sun and the gulls having a look-see.

Minna lies with eyes shut.
Minna lies and listens.
Something rustles.
Minna raises her eyes, and there stand a pair of rubber shoes.
The shoes sit on a pair of feet.
The shoes shuffle uncertainly.
Hair pokes well out from the ankles.
A man has come to Minna's rescue.
Minna can't be bothered.
Minna's not going to be rescued now.
Minna's rescued herself.
Minna props herself up on an elbow: *Yes?*
The man asks, *Are you okay?*
Minna says, *I've been in the water.*
The man hunkers down: *On purpose?*
Minna says, *Not completely.*
The man wants to know if he should call for an ambulance.
Minna places her hands on the rock.
Minna raises herself a bit to sit.
Minna can see the man better now.
The man's plump.
The man has a beard.
Medium height.
The face attractive, and the mouth now opening.
The man says he could hear someone singing.
The man says he crawled out to have a look.
The man's got a banjo on his back.
Minna points at the banjo.
The man looks at the banjo as if it weren't his.
The banjo's his.

The banjo and he were on their way to Årsdale.
The man plays banjo during the tourist season.
Guitar's more for the mainland.
The man introduces himself.
The man says his name's Tim.
Tim seats himself at Minna's side.
Tim sets the banjo up against Minna's backpack.
Tim takes hold of Minna's hand.
Minna's hand is wet and cold.
Tim squeezes the hand a little.
The ambulance isn't out of the picture.
The medicopter isn't either.
Tim raises his index finger.
Tim says Minna should follow it with her eyes.
Tim's finger oscillates, but
Minna has her eye on something else.
The penny's dropped:
*Tim's on Bornholm.*
*Tim's the cousin.*
*Tim knows someone with a rehearsal space in Kastrup.*
*The rehearsal space is cheap.*
Minna can't stop looking.
Tim's family resemblance seeps out.
Tim does look like Lars.
Tim's beard is just more modest.
Tim also looks gentler.
Tim seems nice.
Tim's just about sweet.
Tim is Lars, like Lars was at night.
Tim is Lars without deadlines and Linda.

Lars was a porcupine.
Lars was a pillbox.
Tim's warm and hairy.
Tim's soft and shy.
Tim looks at her worriedly.
Tim says that she's bleeding from her head.
Minna says, *Who isn't?*
Tim says she's freezing, but
Minna isn't freezing.
*It was me who sang*, says Minna
    and then she shoots, she shoots him the mermaid eye.

# QUOTATIONS IN THE TEXT

p. 13 The quotation is a slight paraphrase of “I drill, and either the drill breaks, or else I don’t dare drill deep enough”, from Ingmar Bergman, *Billeder* (*Images*, Copenhagen: Lindhardt og Ringhof, 1990). All quotations from Bergman have been rendered into English by Misha Hoekstra from Danish translations of the original Swedish texts.

p. 17 “Pointlessness grimaces!” in Bergman’s *Laterna Magica* (*Magic Lantern*, Copenhagen: Lindhardt og Ringhof, 1987).

pp. 22–3 and 66 See Jens Peter Jacobsen’s 1874 poem ‘Arabesk: Til en Haandtegning af Michel Angelo’ (‘Arabesque: For a Drawing by Michelangelo’), which begins:

> Did the wave reach land?
> Did it reach land and trickle down slowly,
> Rattling with beads of gravel,
> Back once more into the world of waves?
>
> (Translated from the Danish)

p. 30 Slight simplification of “The ringmaster of a flea circus, as you know, lets the artists suck his blood”, from *Billeder*.

p. 30 “But a daydreamer isn’t an artist except in his dreams”, from *Billeder*.

p. 30 “I contain too much humanity” is the last part of “Here, in my solitude, I have an odd sense that I contain too much humanity”, from *Billeder*.

p. 30 "The days are long, large, light. They're as substantial as cows, as some sort of bloody big animal", from *Billeder*.

p. 40 "You will do what is needed; when nothing is needed, you can't do anything", from *Billeder*.

p. 40 "Failures can have a fresh, bitter taste; the adversity rouses aggression and shakes slumbering creativity awake", from Ingmar Bergman, *Laterna Magica*.

pp. 55 and 66 "Dread makes the dreaded real" is adapted from Bergman's *Laterna Magica,* where it appears as "Dread would soon make the dreaded real".

p. 57 "I pretend to be an adult. Time and again it amazes me that people take me seriously", from *Billeder*.

p. 69 Minna sings Bjørnstjerne Bjørnson's 'Sangen Har Lysning' ('The Song Has Light'), also known as #159 in *Højskolesangbogen* (*The Danish Folk High School Songbook*).

p. 83 Minna sings the last stanza of Carl Orff's 'In Trutina' ('In the Balance'), whose lyric comes from a medieval manuscript. One rendering from the Latin (translator unknown):

> But I choose what I see
> And submit my neck to the yoke:
> I yield to the sweet, sweet yoke.

WINNER OF THE 2014 P.O. ENQUIST LITERARY PRIZE

A *PUBLISHERS WEEKLY* BOOK OF THE YEAR

"To read a Dorthe Nors story is to enter a dream and become subject to its logic . . . Nors knows and understands so much about us; her perceptions frequently shock with their acuity, though within seconds you recognize them as, yes, true"

Daniel Woodrell, award-winning author of *Winter's Bone*

"Reading Dorthe Nors's work, one is reminded of the thrills and dangers of living. Memories, laughter, a gesture: everything casts a shadow, meaningful or mysterious. These stories prove that no loss is too small, and each moment counts"

Yiyun Li, award-winning author of *The Vagrants* and *Kinder Than Solitude*

"Unsettling and poetic . . . Some pieces . . . are oddly beautiful; others are brilliantly disturbing"

*The New York Times*

"Horror and comedy both require timing, and Dorthe Nors has it"

*Chicago Tribune*

"The short-short stories in Danish sensation Nors's slim, potent collection . . . evoke the weirdness and wonder of relating in the digital age"

*Vogue*

"Spare and sublime. Author Dorthe Nors knows how to capture the smallest moments and sculpt them into the unforgettable"

*Oprah*

"Nowhere here is a word out of place . . . Nors's writing doesn't just observe the details of life – online searches, laundry, fantasies, conversations with semi-strangers, compulsions – it offers a marvelous, truthful take on how these details illustrate our souls"

*Publishers Weekly*, starred review

"In the span of two pages, she is able to both build and unmake a character, achieving the same complexity that other writers require entire novels to establish . . . Lovers of the art of literary fiction, students of psychology, and everyone looking for a quick, thought-provoking read should all indulge themselves in the subversive delight of this short story collection"

*Booklist*

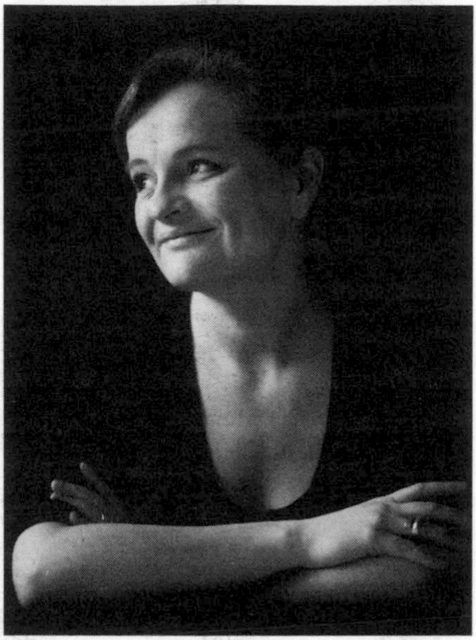

Dorthe Nors was born in 1970 and is one of the most original voices in contemporary Danish literature. She holds a degree in literature and history from Aarhus University and has published four novels so far, in addition to the collection of stories and the novella you are holding in your hand. Nors's short stories have appeared in numerous publications, including *Harper's Magazine* and the *Boston Review*, and she is the first Danish writer ever to have a story published in the *New Yorker*. Nors was awarded the Danish Arts Agency's Three-Year Grant for "her unusual and extraordinary talent" in 2011. In 2014, *Karate Chop* won the prestigious P.O. Enquist Literary Prize.

# KAR
# ATEC
# HOP

Dorthe
Nors

Translated from the Danish
by MARTIN AITKEN

Pushkin Press
71–75 Shelton Street, London WC2H 9JQ



Published by agreement with the Gyldendal Group Agency

*Karate Chop* was first published as *Kantslag* in Denmark in 2008

Stories from this collection first appeared in earlier forms in the following literary journals: "The Wadden Sea" in *AGNI*; "The Buddhist" in the *Boston Review*; "Do You Know Jussi?" in *Ecotone*; "Mutual Destruction" in *FENCE*; "Mother, Grandmother, and Aunt Ellen" in *Guernica*; "Hair Salon" in *Gulf Coast*; "Flight" in *Harper's*; "Duckling" and "She Frequented Cemeteries" in *New Letters*; "The Heron" in the *New Yorker*; "Female Killers" in *The Normal School*; and "The Winter Garden" and "Karate Chop" in *A Public Space*.



This English translation first published in the United States by Graywolf Press in 2014

First published in Great Britain by Pushkin Press in 2015

norden

Nordic Council of Ministers

Supported by a translation grant from the Nordic Council of Ministers

0 0 1

ISBN 978 1 782271 19 2



Set in Sabon Monotype by Tetragon, London

Printed by CPI Group (UK) Ltd, Croydon CR0 4YY

www.pushkinpress.com

*For my parents*

*I come from a home with cats and dogs, and those cats were so much on top you wouldn't believe it. They beat up on the dogs morning, noon, and night. They got beaten up on so much, those dogs, that one year they'd saved up so much hatred they chased one of the neighbor's cats into a tree with the idea of hanging around until it came down again, after which they ate it.*

# CONTENTS

# DO YOU KNOW JUSSI?

SHE CAN HEAR THE OTHERS DOWNSTAIRS. JANUS IS still there too. He has just said good-bye to her up in her room and now he's saying good-bye to her mother in the doorway. Then everything is quiet again, apart from her older brother turning on the shower across the hall. The smell of meatballs has drifted all the way inside her room and she is lying on the bed with a pillow between her knees. She can still feel the wetness of his saliva just beneath her nose, and his fingers. He made an effort to be nice, that was it, and she turns on the TV. She watches what's left of the local news, then finds a show where some person looks for someone they knew who has disappeared.

Tonight it's about a son unable to find his father. The son is thirty, rather chubby, and nearly cries when he says he is not angry with his father. But he can't understand why his father has not written to him. When the girl whose show it is asks if he's sad about that, the son can only nod.

A blond journalist Louise remembers once interviewed the prime minister on the television news is seen going through archives and asking people in public offices for information about the son's missing father. The father's name is uncommon,

Jussi Nielsen, and now the blond journalist is standing outside a redbrick apartment block in a suburb of Copenhagen. He is going to ring the doorbell of an address where someone at the local authority believes Jussi Nielsen may once have lived. *I wonder if anyone's going to be home,* the journalist says as he rings the doorbell. An elderly woman with a short perm opens the door. She doesn't look at the camera when she appears, and she doesn't seem surprised enough when the journalist says he is from national television. *We're looking for a man called Jussi Nielsen,* says the journalist. The woman opens the door a little bit more and says: *Yes, Jussi used to live here.* The journalist nods. *Do you know Jussi?* he asks. *Yes,* says the woman.

It turns out that the woman, whose face Louise finds plain, was once married to Jussi Nielsen, but they got divorced. The way the apartment is done up, Louise can see they most likely never had much in common. But the journalist doesn't care about things like that. He wants to know if the woman knows where Jussi Nielsen is now. The woman smiles, and looks straight into the camera. She looks proud: *Yes, I know where Jussi is,* she says.

Louise knows this is not the time to turn off the TV, but she turns it off anyway. Her brother is tramping about in the hall, but otherwise the place is still quiet. Janus hasn't texted her, but he thought it was a shame it hurt. She looks at the photograph of him by the mirror. He has brown hair and prefers not to smile when his picture is taken. There's one of Mom and Dad on vacation, too. It seems like a long time ago, and she thinks about Jussi Nielsen and about Janus, who is tall. His fingers are slender and attractive, but he always uses

his tongue when he kisses. She finds it odd that he doesn't use his lips once in a while. Tongue is okay, but it reminds her of the time she and her brother went to work with their dad. They licked envelopes for five kroner an hour at either side of a big, oval desk. Being there was all right, apart from the envelopes. She remembers it because she didn't care to look at her brother, who wanted to see whose stack of licked envelopes grew the quickest, so she looked down at her work instead. That way she found herself looking too long at the addresses printed on the envelopes.

The letters were all for men and the addresses made her think about people to whom she didn't belong. She had been able to see them in her mind, going about in strange rooms. She had been able to see them cutting through sports halls, sitting in cars at traffic lights, and walking their bikes and mopeds along the curb. Not just strangers, more like empty sheets of paper waiting to be written on. Or like pausing in front of a butcher's shop window with your mother and seeing the reflection of a man standing next to you. He looks at the pork sausage. He considers buying the pork sausage, the strange man at the window. Then he decides not to. He turns away, and just before he disappears around the corner he stops and gives you and your mother a strange look.

She had imagined it like that, and she had imagined how she followed the man through the streets all the way to his door, into his stairway and up to the second floor. She went with him inside his apartment and into the kitchen. Here the man made coffee and adjusted the photograph on the counter. Then he went into the living room and turned on the television and watched the news.

She had watched the man as he sat rubbing the armrests with his thumbs. She watched him during the television news, watched him as he ate his pork chops. Later, she was there when he went to the bathroom, and in the ambience of the bedroom when the man put down his magazine on the bedside table and reached out to turn off the light.

There he had lain under his white linen, smelling of duvet, and Louise had wanted to cry. She wanted to shake the man and ask if he had a car. Because if he had a car she wanted him to take her home. She didn't want to be there anymore. She wanted to go home to her mother, but she couldn't, because this man, who was nothing but a name on an envelope, had stuck to her, and when later she rang all the doorbells on the stairway to ask if they knew anything about the man who lived on the second floor, they all said they didn't. His name could have been Olsen, Madsen, Hansen, or Nielsen. No one knew.

"Are you okay? Do you want me to fetch Dad?" her brother had asked that day at their father's office when they had licked envelopes, and at that moment Louise remembers saying she didn't care for the adhesive.

"My stomach feels odd," she said, and then her brother fetched their dad.

But that was then, she thinks to herself, and slides her fingers under her panties to where the skin is thin. It still feels tender, but she thinks it will pass. Her mother is filling the dishwasher, and Dad turns up the volume on the late-night news. She mutes the phone and closes her eyes. No word from Janus. That's a strange name too.

# MUTUAL DESTRUCTION

HE WHISTLES HIS DOG TO HIM, PUTS A COLLAR ON IT, and pulls it a short way back from the edge of the wood so they're not stuck out like a sore thumb. It's late in the day and there's a big fallow field between him and Morten, so he can remain standing here. Morten is going about the farmyard with the red bitch at his heels. It's lean and rough haired, and he's always only ever had dachshunds. Small, aggressive animals that chew the lead and the floor mats in the car, and Henrik doesn't like small dogs. But when they go hunting foxes, Morten takes his dachshund, and when they go shooting by the fjord, Henrik takes his small munsterlander and the decoys. They've sat many times in the caravan on the Gardeners' land down in the bog, drinking weak coffee from plastic cups, the air dense with the smell of wet dog, talking about how practically things divided up, Henrik having a big dog for the one thing and Morten having dachshunds for the other. But now Morten's down there in the farmyard alone. A single light is shining from the kitchen window. He must have forgotten to switch it off, and the dog reaches only to his bootlegs. It looks like he's trying to fix some part of the door in the gable wall. There's a lot needs fixing now. There's a lot needs to sink in.

Henrik, for instance, always thought it was the wife's fault, because she gave you the feeling that one of the things she liked best about Morten was that he wasn't good enough. It can't have been easy for Morten, being married to someone who was always looking for the horizons in everything. She talked big, and Morten must have felt awkward about the students at school calling her Skylark, and you can see it in the house down there as well. The windows are the sort with narrow wooden bars and they're painted red like in Sweden. There's some wickerwork by the main door, and when you come in it's all long tables in the living room and hand-sewn cushions, and on the walls what they called expressive art.

You always ended up feeling a bit wrong when you visited Morten and his wife. Tina, in particular, came across as the kind of person who had nothing against sticking her hand into a duck and pulling out the gizzard. It was because she was brought up in the country. She knew how most things looked on the inside. And she wasn't bothered if it smelled, as long as it was useful for something. She didn't mind taking her turn and getting her hands dirty, but Morten's wife was one who hoarded from her surroundings. Things had to have diplomas, titles, and certificates. Even Morten's dogs had to have pedigrees and long names, but Morten liked that about her. And he thought she looked fantastic with her schoolbag, her blond hair, and her little smocks. He liked that his dogs, which he called Muggi and Molly and Sif so as not to be laughed at, underneath had sophisticated names. One of them was called Ariadne Pil-Neksø. The last part after a kennel in Northern Jutland, and Morten liked to say how much Ariadne Pil-Neksø had cost, but Ariadne Pil-Neksø had never been able to flush

a fox out of its hole, and Henrik shot it on the little patch of land behind the house while it was digging in a molehill.

Like it should be, he thinks to himself and puts his hand down to his big dog. It's twilight, and its wet tongue licks the palm of his hand. He watches his hunting pal going about the yard, back and forth, with what looks like an electric drill. Morten has his dog with him, too. A lively little thing, all instinct, but basically slight and always in danger of coming out worst. This strange bond between dog and hunter, he feels unable to put it into words, but maybe it's something like crossing piss streams, and it's why a hunter should always be able to shoot his own dog. That's the way it is: shoot your best friend, but know your limits, too. That was how Morten had put it back then, almost ten years ago when they'd been sitting in the kitchen and he'd said that the dog he had then had cancer.

"You've to know when you've not got it in you," Morten had said. "If you shoot this one, I'll take yours when its turn comes."

He'd gestured with a finger at Henrik's first hunting dog. Such a lovely big dog, lying there in front of the radiator looking up at him.

They'd agreed to keep it to themselves, and he shot Morten's dog, the one with cancer, as promised, and three years later Morten shot the first of his. They were quits then, for the next of Henrik's died all by itself. But it had been different with Morten's, and nothing wrong with that. From the dog's point of view, and the hunter's, a clean shot was the best thing. It wouldn't be right for an animal to be crammed inside a car and driven to the vet. A clean shot when the dog's doing something

it likes is a good death for a dog. He wouldn't mind going that way himself one day when he was as far up in Tina as he could get. That'd suit him fine, but still he's standing here at the edge of the wood with an unpleasant feeling inside him while Morten goes about the yard in a way that makes it plain his wife and children are gone. It can't have come as much of a surprise, though. Everyone had known for years she was the leaving kind. Everyone had thought for years that Morten looked so small alongside her. It had always been good company in the Gardeners' caravan, even though Morten had become such a bigmouth. They'd always been friends, but there was a lack of balance in it. He had never let him down. He shot the first of Morten's dogs as it came up out of a foxhole. The next one he shot in the plantation with the Christmas trees. The third had been in such pain for some reason; Morten said it had been run over, but it could just as well have been something else entirely. It was so bad Henrik had to lay it in place for the shot, and the dog with the stupid name he took care of on the little patch behind the house. The fifth he shot in the back garden one day when the wife wasn't home, but now it was the last of them, the last dachshund, going about the yard at Morten's heels down there. A man and his dog in the twilight, but something more. He had to take it in. Take a good look, because that's how it was: there was something inside Morten that shunned the light. Something Tina said was a kind of complex. He didn't know what it was. He didn't know what to say about it, other than that it smelled like offal, and that the smell was spreading.

# THE BUDDHIST

BEFORE THE BUDDHIST BECAME PRESIDENT OF THE AID organization People to People, he was an ordinary Christian and a government official in the Ministry of Foreign Affairs. He was the one who wrote the foreign minister's speeches and thereby put words into the foreign minister's mouth. It was a way of lying and at first it didn't bother him any. Then it started bugging him because he realized he was a Buddhist. It didn't come to him all of a sudden that he was a Buddhist. It was more like the Buddhist, as an idea, crept up and settled in him shortly after his wife said she wanted a divorce. The Buddhist came in and sat down at the opposite side of his desk at the Ministry of Foreign Affairs. He contemplated the Buddhist and thought it was a good format to step into. Buddhists are good people. They're deeper than most. Buddhists can see connections no one else can. These were all qualities he recognized in himself, but which all could be improved upon, and so he became a Buddhist. If he hadn't become a Buddhist, the divorce would have hurt that much more, but a Buddhist gains insight through pain. The more it hurts, the wiser the Buddhist becomes, the government official thought, and stopped being a Lutheran.

Shortly after the Buddhist has divorced and become a Buddhist, he stands in front of the mirror looking at his face beneath

his thin, mousy hair. His skin is pale, but the exterior isn't what matters. The Dalai Lama would never lie on behalf of a government minister, and he would never tell international lies. More importantly, the Dalai Lama would never shy from pain. The Dalai Lama smiles when things hurt, and the more burdened the Dalai Lama, the more the world senses the Dalai Lama's presence. *Aim high,* the Buddhist thinks to himself, and decides to write an article in a national newspaper. The article is about his place of work, the Ministry of Foreign Affairs. More than that, it is about the lies that issue from the mouth of the foreign minister. *The prime minister is a thief, and the foreign minister is a liar. I should know, because I'm the one who writes the speeches,* the Buddhist writes in the newspaper, and the next day he is not afraid to go to work. Resistance builds character, and because the Buddhist is a government official employed by the state, the foreign minister cannot dismiss the Buddhist from his position. However, the permanent undersecretary can ride the elevator and have serious words with him, which is what he does. Up and down, up and down. Up and down with the Buddhist at the Ministry of Foreign Affairs.

Shortly after the article and the elevator ride with the permanent undersecretary, the Buddhist's situation looks like this: he is divorced. At his request he has been granted leave of absence from his position in the Ministry of Foreign Affairs. And now there are three things hurting. The foreign minister hurts. His wife wanting to sell the big house in Charlottenlund hurts. And last but not least, it hurts that his aptitude for implementing lasting change in the world, both as a Buddhist and as a former

government official in the Ministry of Foreign Affairs, is not being put to use. His desire to do good is overwhelming. His need to implement positive change in the world around him keeps him awake at nights. He drives around Copenhagen, anxious to get to work and ready to adapt. He drives around in his red Citroën Berlingo and keeps an eye on his wife. He drives around in his red Citroën Berlingo and keeps an eye on the foreign minister. He wishes both of them well. Yet he also wants to do them harm. It's a paradox, but the Buddhist loves them both while at the same time wanting to harm them. *I want to harm them,* he says out loud to himself, and just at the very moment he hears the word *harm* rush between his teeth, he sees himself in the rearview mirror. What he sees there is a Buddhist. *A good thing I'm a Buddhist,* he thinks to himself. *God knows what I might have done if I hadn't been a Buddhist.*

But he is a Buddhist, and Buddhists have expanding souls. He drives around in the affluence of northern Copenhagen in the night and learns that it is the Buddhist inside him who is stronger. Inside him is an abundance of goodness. He can sense this is good, and he senses how meaningful it all is. The Universe is plotting coordinates for him. The Universe wants something from him. If the Universe hadn't wanted something from him, then (a) his wife would never have left him, and (b) the Ministry of Foreign Affairs would never have pressured him into quitting. There is a meaning behind everything, and the Buddhist has had the feeling for a long time that he is the kind of person who is able to grasp the meaning behind things. He has also had the feeling for a long time that the world needs a strong, solitary man to save it. He is a Buddhist

and a former government official in the Ministry of Foreign Affairs. Two birds with one stone. He is a Buddhist, a former government official, and used to lying. Three in one.

It is not long before the Buddhist sees an advertisement in a national newspaper and takes it to be yet another sign from the Universe. The aid organization People to People, based in the city of Aarhus, is looking for a president. *Aha,* thinks the Buddhist, who at this point is also a divorced, unemployed subtenant in an apartment in the South Harbor district of Copenhagen. *Aha,* he thinks, *an organization is a good place to begin if you want to change the world.*

There are two reasons why an organization is a good place to begin changing the world. First, an organization sells convictions rather than products. Second, selling convictions is all about ideals. The Buddhist has plenty of ideals. But that's not all. Ideals attract young people and other idealists. The young people and the idealists are all going to work for the Buddhist and the Cause. He can pretty much decide for himself what the Cause is going to be, as long as it involves *people* and *aid*. Both things appeal to him. It would be good to have a world in which everyone was equally fat; not too fat, but happy. The Buddhist decides in his sublet apartment in the South Harbor that he wants to be president of the aid organization People to People. He also decides to call the volunteer workers World Ambassadors. The Buddhist wants to be their boss, or even better: he wants to be their leader.

To get the job he must lie. No, put that another way: to get the job he must put words into his own mouth. Which is

allowed in a good cause, and he has lots of experience at it. He puts together a good, inaccurate letter of application. He has no problem omitting the fact that he is actually no longer married to the woman named as his wife. He has no problem either with his mail being redirected from the address in Charlottenlund. Removing various sticking points from his résumé is easy, and when it is done he sends the application. If he lies awake on his inflatable mattress on the floor in the South Harbor apartment, it is not because he has lied. He has accepted that the end justifies the means. If he lies awake it's because he is tense thinking whether there is any way the organization's board of directors can get around him. Which of course there isn't. The chairman of the board is convinced as soon as he opens the envelope and sees the letterhead of the Ministry of Foreign Affairs. The board is in complete agreement, and calls the Buddhist right away. The board likes the sound of the Buddhist's voice on the telephone. The board likes the way the Buddhist is "ready to drive to Aarhus immediately." At the interview the board likes the way he drinks water from his glass. It likes the sound of his wedding ring when it chinks against the glass and taps against the desk. It likes his commitment to the problems of the world. It likes his dreams of a bigger, stronger People to People. The Buddhist is a visionary. The Buddhist is a family man. The Buddhist once held a diplomatic passport. The board has never seen the like. It is dazzled and ought to be wearing sunglasses. The Buddhist is more than convincing. There was, as the board would later state, "absolutely no getting around him." Or, as the female member of the board told a reporter from the Aarhus daily: *He wore leather elbow*

*patches. We thought he was an intellectual.* But she doesn't say that until later.

We are now at the point at which the Buddhist becomes the leader of a movement, and it is at this point, just prior to his relocating, that he acquires his puppy dog. The puppy dog is a black Labrador and he calls it Sancho. Buddhists are kind to animals, and leadership is about incorporating soft values into work structures, and Sancho is soft. The Buddhist puts the dog on the floor of his Berlingo, and drives away from the South Harbor. The Buddhist is on his way to Aarhus with plans for his life and for the world. He has an inflatable mattress on the rear seat and ten pairs of clean underpants. He has plans for the world and the key to a provided residence in Aarhus. He is the new president of the aid organization People to People and he has been in the newspapers. He is driving toward a greater future than the one he envisaged before. He is driving toward the kind of future that women will appreciate. Who knows, he may even meet the foreign minister one day on a plantation in some developing country with himself as host for the whole thing. He smiles at the thought and stops the car only when Sancho needs to urinate. He himself is a Buddhist and urinates only when he wants to.

At a rest area west of Odense while the dog is urinating he happens to look at his car, the Berlingo. He thinks about how it is just the right car for him. From headlight to tailgate the Berlingo signals roominess. The design of this particular model with its sliding rear doors makes it easier to get in and out with schoolbags, groceries, and the desire to make a difference in

the world. You couldn't say the Berlingo was a sexy car, the Buddhist thinks. But that's okay, because the Berlingo is meant to signal inner, rather than outer, values. The design is meant to indicate that the owner is practical, reliable, and flexible. The fact that the Berlingo is a safe car is hardly immaterial either. Around the cabin is a metal frame said to be so solid that nothing bad can ever get to anyone inside.

The Buddhist puts the dog on the floor of the car again and as he drives away from the rest area he realizes that the Berlingo is yet another sign from the Universe. He is driving the safest car on the market. He is driving a car in which no one can die. But even though dangerous things like death can't get into the Berlingo from the outside, that doesn't mean danger is not already inside the car. It strikes the Buddhist that if he were a force of evil in the world, then he would be afraid of himself. *If I were evil, I would hate me,* the Buddhist thinks. *And if I were someone who wanted to do good in the world, what car would I choose?* the Buddhist asks himself as he overtakes a Volvo with Swedish license plates. It's a hypothetical question. The Buddhist has already chosen the Berlingo.

It appears a short moment after he overtakes the Volvo: the omen. The Buddhist receives an omen, and the omen manifests itself above the Lillebælt Bridge, which he is approaching. In the sky over Fredericia, or perhaps even the whole region, he sees a great halo. The closer he gets to the Lillebælt Bridge, the brighter the halo becomes. The moment the wheels of the Berlingo touch the Lillebælt Bridge, the gray metal of the Lillebælt Bridge is transformed into a shining Bifröst arching across the strait and stretching up into the sky. It is like a

mirage and yet quite real. The Buddhist is driving on an astral body and he is heading in the direction of the heavens. Down in Denmark, far below him, people scurry out into their gardens and point up at him and the Berlingo. They point at the red Berlingo driving across the sky as though it were Halley's Comet. The Buddhist feels the energy rushing into him from the Universe and lets himself be driven in great sweeping arcs through the clouds. He waves at Denmark below, and parts of northern Germany, and then eventually he arrives at a shining gateway. He does not inquire of himself whether he is supposed to drive through the gateway. He is the Chosen One. The whole meaning of the gateway is for him to drive through it, and so he does. He drives until the car stops all by itself, high above central Jutland. He takes the dog under his arm, opens the door, and steps out into the heavens. He can walk on the clouds. He cannot fall, and he senses a figure in orange garments, with a clean-shaven head and large spectacles coming toward him. There is no need to look closer; it is obviously the Lama. The Buddhist kneels and hopes that the dog will not urinate at this hallowed moment. He doesn't dare to lift his head. He feels like a pixie and wants to tell the Lama so, but he doesn't dare to look at him. He thinks that if pure goodness looks at pure goodness something might explode. *Thank you,* he says simply. *Thank you for your goodness and wisdom,* and the Lama lays his hand on his head and replies: *Don't mention it, my boy, and remember now, you need chaos in your soul to give birth to a dancing star.*

It is in this scene, which may have taken place in the skies above Jutland, or perhaps somewhere far inside the Buddhist, that we

must look for the reason why the Buddhist, four months later, locks himself inside his office with a jerry can full of gasoline and a disposable lighter. It is here that we meet him again. He is sitting at his desk staring beyond the jerry can and yet hardly noticing the room that encloses him. He is locked inside a mental cage. No one can get in, and the chairman of the board wants to speak to the Buddhist. The Buddhist is being dismissed from his position for abuse of office, deceit, negligence, firing people on emotional grounds, creative accounting, manipulating subscription figures, misappropriating public funds, having sex with his subordinates, and similar improprieties. But most of all, the Buddhist is being dismissed on account of his ravings and the trail of chaos he has left behind him through the aid organization People to People. He is being dismissed for having made a charitable organization his plaything, for having big ideas about himself, and he is being allowed to resign nicely if he wants. Discreetly, and with the right to concoct a story. But he is being dismissed, and he won't go. It's not because he loves his work that he won't go. It's because going just isn't an option. None of the great mavericks could ever have been dismissed: Stalin, Hitler, Mother Teresa, Nelson Mandela, the Dalai Lama. He has no qualms about uttering these names in the same breath. They have a lot in common. None of them could have been dismissed, for instance. The Buddhist has locked himself inside his office with the gasoline, the dog, his ex-wife's phone number, and the female board member tied to a chair with the minutes of a meeting in her mouth. He has locked himself in with his dream of a better world and a jerry can from the Statoil station around the corner. He has locked himself in with his goodness, and the rest is history.

# THE WINTER GARDEN

IT WAS THE NIGHT DIRCH PASSER THE COMEDIAN DIED. He collapsed onstage. His heart was sick and he was taken away by ambulance to the hospital, where they said he was dead on arrival. It was September 3, 1980, and the reason I remember it so well is that it was the night my mother and father decided to tell me they were getting divorced. This was announced during dinner and somewhere inside me I think I was relieved. It may sound harsh, but they didn't match, so when Mom told me, all I did was put down my fork. By ten o'clock the news was out about Dirch Passer. Those two things, his death and me standing by the porch door looking out on the moss Dad always let grow between the paving stones, are inseparable to me.

The first year and a half, I lived with my mother and visited Dad in his new row house every two weeks. He never really got moved in, my father. He slept on a daybed in the big bedroom and we ate chicken from the hamburger stand when I was there. Then what happened was that Mom found a boyfriend. His name was Henning, he was alone with two daughters, and we would sit in the living room playing cards in the evening. My father was sad when I visited him. He kept saying to me

that it didn't matter. What? I asked him. Nothing, he said, and then I talked to Mom and Henning about it maybe being fair, seeing how Henning's two daughters lived with them, that I moved into the spare room at my father's.

It was June 6, 1982, and as we sat in the car outside Dad's house my mother kept pulling down the sleeves of my jersey and saying that I should know there was a way back. She stepped inside with me, no more than that, and that was how I got the spare room at my father's. He'd tried to make the place nice. The furniture was pushed back against the walls, and there was a coffee table with a large ashtray in the living room. He'd bought bookshelves, too, and in his bedroom there was a narrow bed the same as the one he had put in the spare room for me. My room was all cleaned and it was plenty big enough. I don't know where he got the drapes from, but he pulled them together so I could see they worked.

There were good and bad things that summer I lived with Dad. One good thing was the World Cup in Spain. Paolo Rossi was the top scorer with six goals, and the Northern Ireland striker Norman Whiteside was the youngest player ever in the finals at seventeen years and forty-one days. We watched the games together, Dad and me, and because the sun was beating down outside we had all the drapes closed. The dark living room, the smell of relish, and the warm television set were good things. But then when we went out together, like to the supermarket, Dad couldn't help but put his arm round my neck to show that we belonged together, though nobody else could care less.

Dad had been lucky to get the house, he said, and he was especially happy about the patio enclosure. It would be warm

out there even in winter, so Dad filled it up with desert plants and called it the winter garden. Whereas the living room, the kitchen, and the bathroom seemed big, the winter garden was soft and cozy. Sometimes in the evenings if there was nothing on television he would want us to sit out there in garden chairs and talk. He grew succulent plants and onions and fed them with plant food so they grew really big. He had a Crassula, as he called it, that was five feet tall. I was to have it one day, because I happened to say it was the most beautiful. Sometimes to make him happy I said that the warm earth in the winter garden smelled like the jungle. Other times I said his plants were so big he looked like Tarzan when he was standing among them. Then he would laugh and call me Korak, but before he and Mom divorced, he had no hobbies.

I could definitely have gone on living with my father, but then what happened was that in the middle of September that year a divorced lady from my father's work discovered that he was divorced, too. Her name was Margit. I saw her one day out in the winter garden going back and forth with a glass of white wine in her hand. While my father was explaining to her how the succulent plants stored water inside them like camels, I saw how she was looking at the wallpaper in the living room. And then she invited Dad and me to her home one Sunday afternoon. It was September 30, 1982, the day Dirch Passer's national health card would have expired if he had been alive, and the thing I remember most from that day is that this woman Margit had a son.

He sat on the couch staring sullenly at me. I stared back to make him stop. He stuck his tongue out at my father when he wasn't looking. That may seem like a petty thing, but it was

only then I realized that I was the only person who thought my father was someone special. It was only my way of looking at him that stopped him from being just some ordinary guy of no importance who could be replaced by any other ordinary guy of no importance. If I didn't like him he would basically be insignificant, and if he were insignificant, things would look pretty bad for me. So I cut everything I felt for my father into pieces and hid them away where best I could. In my thoughts, I mean. Some went underneath the table in the living room; some went into Margit's houseplants and into the ugly mouth of her son. That way the boy would have to find it all again before he could stick his tongue out at it.

I don't know what happened between my father and this Margit woman that day, but I never saw her again, and when we left there was no time for me to put all the pieces I had hidden together again. Outside in the car, where I sat up front, I remember I didn't care to look at my father at first. But then I did anyway and it was true. There was just a guy driving a car and I stuck my tongue out at him when he wasn't looking.

# THE BIG TOMATO

THE BANGS WORK A LOT AND NEVER SHOP FOR groceries themselves. Everything in the refrigerator is ordered online. Every Sunday evening they place their order. Every Monday a box is left outside the door with all their food. One of these Mondays the box contains a tomato weighing more than four pounds, which the Bangs do not believe they ordered. The first thing is that they cannot possibly eat a tomato that big. The other thing is that they are paying by the ounce. It's too expensive, says Mrs. Bang, so Mr. Bang calls the online grocery store to complain. At seven that evening, while I am busy in the guest bathroom, the doorbell rings. As usual, Mr. and Mrs. Bang are not at home and it's up to me to see who it is. A small man is standing there sweating and says he has come to collect the tomato. I fetch it from the refrigerator and give it to him.

He remains standing on the mat, so I ask him if there is anything else. He says he doesn't get paid for his work, other than what he makes in tips from the customers. I explain to him that the Bangs are not at home. He says he picks up his deliveries on a bike that has no brakes. He shows me the soles of his shoes and wipes his forehead.

Mr. and Mrs. Bang are very nice people. Mrs. Bang works for the Danish Consulate on Second Avenue, organizing trade delegations from her home country. Mr. Bang, or Lars, as he likes to be called, is a record producer. I got this job cleaning their penthouse in Lower Manhattan because I do the cleaning in his record studio. Mrs. Bang is very tall and beautiful and has blond hair. Mr. Bang is even taller, and if he is home when I arrive he gives me a high-five with his hand down low. The nameplate on the door says the Great Danes. This is a joke by some friends of theirs. I like the Bangs, but when the Bangs aren't at home I'm always afraid they will suddenly appear in the doorway.

That's why I hesitate to invite the man inside. But he is sweating, and the Bangs have air-conditioning. I tell him my name is Raquel and that he must take off his shoes. His name is Gabriel. He says he has other returns he needs to pick up elsewhere in the city. I tell him I'll give him something for his trouble. He says he won't accept anything if it's my own money. We smile, and he puts the tomato down carefully on the kitchen counter.

"I don't know what to give you," I say, but then he says I can let him freshen up a little.

The Bangs have a separate bathroom for guests, but my buckets and cleaning supplies are in there and the Bangs never told me what to do about guests like Gabriel. So I indicate the sink in the kitchen and he pulls the sleeves of his T-shirt up over his shoulders. Gabriel washes like my father used to in the kitchen at home in Puerto Consol. Mexican men lather themselves up to the elbows and pay special attention to the eyes and ears and nose. And when they rinse the soap away

they snort like the first Mexican snorted as he staggered out of the Rio Grande. This is how Gabriel washes, and when he is done he half turns to face me. I hurry into the guest bathroom to get him a towel. The dirty ones are in a pile on the floor. The clean ones from Lumturi are folded in a neat stack. I take a clean one and go back to the kitchen where he stands dripping.

"I could make you a sandwich," I tell him as I hand him the towel.

"I don't want to be any trouble," he says.

I point at the tomato and say:

"*Es un jitomate muy grande, pero no puede bajar las escaleras por si mismo.*"*

While he eats his sandwich I finish up my cleaning in the guest bathroom, and when I'm done scouring the bowl I put the dirty towels and the Bangs' bed linen in the laundry bag for Lumturi. In the kitchen, Gabriel is standing in his stockinged feet looking at the bulletin board.

"They are tall people, right?"

He indicates how tall he thinks the Bangs would be beside him if they were at home.

He is looking at some photos from the Bangs' wedding. There are quite a few on the bulletin board, and I tell him that the people who live here are from Denmark. He looks at the photo of the Bangs together with a lot of other people outside a small, white church. Everyone looks tall, though not as tall as Mr. and Mrs. Bang. Another photo shows them in wedding outfits standing by a horse-drawn carriage in front of a castle in a sumptuous green landscape. Mrs. Bang's hair

* *It's a very big tomato, but it can't go down the stairs on its own.*

has been put up in a way that makes her look even taller. In another photo, Mr. Bang is carrying her over his shoulder. She is so high up her head is not even in the picture.

Gabriel repeats what he said about them being tall. I tell him that the Bangs are nice people, which is true. Then Gabriel points at the horse-drawn carriage and says he thinks it's strange for people to come to America when they have lives like in that picture. I say ordinary people may find it hard to understand, but even people like the Bangs will live abroad if it means their lives can be happier.

I point to the blue laundry bag and tell Gabriel not to forget the tomato. I am done here. We take the stairs together without speaking. Outside the evening is warm and his bike is where he left it. It has a large box, and he has the key. He puts the tomato inside next to some other vegetables, but I don't notice what kind. Then he bends down and turns the pedals with his hand. He scratches his head. Eventually he straightens up, takes the laundry bag out of my hand, and puts it on top of the box.

"I'm going your way," he says.

He pushes the bike along beside me and we head for Snowy White. Lumturi, the Albanian laundryman, never closes. As we walk, Gabriel tells me his brother sells unsalted bread and holiday flowers in a Jewish neighborhood in Brooklyn. I tell him that's not far from where I live. He says his bike is borrowed and he has been promised a job with a car to drive. I tell him I live with my cousin who isn't married either, and then I point to the laundry shop on the other side of the street.

"Take the tomato out of the box and come in with me," I tell him. "Lumturi never saw such a big tomato in all his life."

Lumturi is fastening the hem of a dress. He looks up at me and smiles when we walk in. I put the laundry bag on the counter and show him the tomato.

"Did you ever see one that big?"

Lumturi puts his hands to his face as if the tomato gave him a scare.

"Where did it come from?"

"It's from the Bangs. The laundry is theirs, too."

"May I?"

Gabriel places the tomato in Lumturi's outstretched hands. It looks funny, Lumturi standing there cradling it as if it were a baby. We sit down for a while and Lumturi tells us about his homeland, how it was like a foggy morning. You go out anyway, because a man needs to walk even if he has no idea where he is going. He walks all day and the fog does not lift until evening, leaving the man standing in the middle of nowhere. He scans the horizon for life, but there is none. He looks back over his shoulder toward the house that isn't there. Tired legs and no place to go with yourself, that's what it was like where he came from, Lumturi says. He hands the tomato back to Gabriel, carefully, as though it were his.

When we leave the Laundromat we don't know which direction to go. I ask Gabriel if he needs to deliver the tomato somewhere. He says all the groceries people don't want are taken to a cold store in the Meatpacking District. He asks where I'm headed, and I tell him home.

"To them?" he asks, gesturing in the air.

"No, home to myself," I say, and point toward the Brooklyn Bridge.

Gabriel thinks it will be okay to take the tomato back in

the morning. We can walk over the bridge together. There's a walkway across the top, and cars and boats beneath. Far off to our right is the Statue of Liberty, which is small and green, and I tell Gabriel how I like my paella. He tells me they grew oranges back home. We talk about the things we miss, warm sand especially, and we discover we both used to tie string to cockroaches and take them for walks when we were kids.

Halfway across the bridge I make him turn around so we can look back at where we have come from. We stare at the Manhattan skyline, which is like it always is. He adjusts my cardigan at the shoulder. I smile, and he pulls gently on my little finger.

"*Es tan pequeño,*" he says and gives it a squeeze.

Then our fingers interlock, and somewhere over Manhattan fireworks are going off. Two spheres light up the sky. They look like faces smiling. Like a kind of happiness so big it can't all be in the picture. The fireworks explode above our heads, above the river and the skyscrapers. Gabriel tries to tell me something, but I can't hear him. I take the handlebars of his bike and we cross the bridge. He and I and the tomato.

# DUCKLING

ALONGSIDE THE BIG FARM, DAD RAN A DUCK FARM, and because he was a clever man he earned a lot of money from it. It helped, too, that he was orderly and always had a good grip on things. He liked that. He was known for saying, whenever anyone brought something up that had already been discussed, that he thought that had all been squared away. It didn't matter whether it was me or my sister, a business acquaintance or just a neighbor he'd been talking politics with, he'd always say: I thought we'd got that all squared away. He'd say it to Mom whenever anything came between them, just like he'd say it to his other women whenever they got distraught about him not wanting a divorce.

I remember one time one of the others came to the house. I was sitting up in the gable window where I could see everything. A car came, and this little woman got out. Mom wasn't home, and I couldn't hear what Dad was saying at first. He was standing on the step and she was by the hood of the car talking in a sharp voice about tidying up after yourself. I would have closed the window but I was too scared, and then he said it to her, that he thought they'd got all that squared away. I don't think she said anything in reply. She just took this not very big plastic bag from the backseat of the car and gave it to him and then drove off.

That was the first time I saw one of the women Dad had on the side. Actually, it was the only time, but Mom said he had several and that it all came in periods. At his funeral years later, I was too scared to look up from the hole for fear that there'd be all these women I didn't know standing around it too. I looked at the lid of the coffin instead and told myself there was only the close family and the priest. I didn't want to think about what Dad looked like in the coffin. And I didn't want to think about what he would look like in time. Fluids can seep in anywhere, and the body means something to those left behind.

Obviously I was a bit quiet for a time after seeing the business with the other woman from the window in the gable. Dad could detect things. He was sharp, and he was watching the expressions on my face. Then one evening not long afterward he looked at my sister during dinner and said that a man with a wife had no business sleeping with women outside his marriage. Not if there were feelings involved. If there were no feelings, there was no problem. Man was like any other animal who had to have his basic needs fulfilled. He had no respect for girls who went to bed with men on the first night, and he had no respect for men who beat their wives. My sister sat looking into her glass of water while Dad said that a woman shouldn't have a deep voice either. And it was no good if she tried to be funny. She was allowed to be subtle. But a woman trying to be funny was compensating for being fat or ugly in some other way. A woman who knew she was good looking and for that reason could afford to keep quiet was a completely different thing.

That's what he said, and then my sister drank her water and looked across at me. There wasn't much in it that was

new. Dad had his boxes and he put things away in them, even things that contradicted each other. But I remember afterward when the table had been cleared. We were sitting in the living room watching television. He prodded me on the knee and pointed to Mom, who had fallen asleep in the armchair. Her chin had dropped onto her chest, and she was twitching just beneath the skin every time her muscles relaxed. Dad smiled then and said: The way she's sitting there, you can see that Mom's really just an animal.

But he was fond of Mom. He couldn't have lived without her, because men couldn't, he said. Men had to have wives, and my sister and I still talk about how moved he was at their twenty-fifth anniversary. He'd already lost a lot of weight then and there he was making a toast to Mom and looking down at her. He said he'd be a goner without her, and we were so fond of him. When I think about memories of him I've lots. We never wanted for anything, and my sister and I were allowed to do all sorts of things. I remember him tow-starting cars, and I remember when we were snowed in and he got us out. I remember the feeling of being held up high and thrown into the air without knowing if I'd be caught again. For me happiness will always be the feeling of landing in his arms.

I especially remember how he hatched the ducklings in a big hatching machine that smelled of warm eggs and feathers. Sometimes he'd hold the eggs up to his ear and shake them to see if there was any life. If there wasn't he'd let me throw them in among the trees, and the other ones he put back. When the ducklings were about to hatch, a little hole would appear in the egg. Then you could see the duckling pecking away in there. It was always an excitement to see if they'd

survive. If they couldn't stand and walk properly Dad would bash them hard against the floor. I remember once he gave me this weedy little duckling. He said I could see if I could keep it alive. I came up with the idea that the oven would have the same effect as the hatching machine. I took a little box and lined it with a floor cloth. I put the duckling inside and put the box in the oven. I don't know what I set the oven on, but it wasn't more than fifty degrees. Then I closed the oven door and sat down in front of the glass. Of course it died eventually, and he was kind and said I shouldn't be upset. Ducklings like that almost always died eventually. We buried it together behind the machine shed in a plastic bag, and he let me fill up the hole myself.

# FEMALE KILLERS

WHEN SHE GOES TO BED, WHICH IS EARLIER AND EARLIER now, he stays up at the computer. He checks the weather, reads an online tabloid, and plays backgammon with someone who says he's a retiree. Who wins is an open issue, and shortly after midnight the retiree logs off. So then he surfs around, visiting a variety of websites, these days thinking about things he hasn't thought about since he was a child. People who can predict things. Clocks that stop when someone dies. Calves with two heads, and women who kill people. The latter is an anomaly, and yet he has noticed that perpetrators in TV crime shows are most often women. He knows it's a technical thing: a desire to surprise the viewer. In the real world it's men who kill, but even when he googles killers, Aileen Wuornos crops up everywhere, and she's a scary one.

Her upbringing was full of violence and alcohol, and at the age of thirteen she was pregnant. No one knew who the father was, most likely not even Aileen herself, who claimed to have had many sexual partners, including her grandfather and her brother. The child to which Aileen gave birth was placed for adoption and Aileen worked as a prostitute through school, her destructive behavior gathering momentum with charges of drunk driving, assault, and unlawful possession of firearms. Aileen ended up earning money as a highway hooker

using names like Sandra, Cammie, and Susan at truck stops in Florida. Her first victim was an electrician. His car was found not far from the freshwater swamps of Tomoka State Park. In the grass by the car they found his empty wallet, some unused condoms, and a half-empty bottle of vodka. A few days later they found the electrician himself, shot three times in the chest with a .22-caliber pistol. After that she went crazy. That must have been it, he thinks to himself, with the same feeling he had when he was a child and dug up the dead birds after he had found and buried them.

They gave Aileen Wuornos six life sentences, one for each man they could prove she killed, and toward the end of her incarceration she claimed her brain was being controlled by radio waves and she would be kidnapped by angels in a spaceship: *I'd just like to say I'm sailing with the Rock,* was the last thing she said before they gave her the injection. *I'll be back, like Independence Day with Jesus. Big mother ship and all, I'll be back.*

The odd thing about Aileen is that she was the kind of person you could have had fun with in a bar when you were young, if the chance came around. Maybe that's why she opens doors in the mind. Doors, stairwells, and pantries. She makes tracks through the undergrowth, to places with abandoned cars. He can smell the soil and rust when he thinks about her. It's okay, though not unambiguously so, because it feels like an opening along the breastbone, and out of the opening seeps everything a person is not supposed to touch: vipers, game killed in traffic, and liver spots. He thinks too about the child she gave up for adoption when she was thirteen. That child has to be out there somewhere, and he imagines him grown

up and coming back from the public office where you can get information on your biological parents. Aileen Wuornos, the birth certificate would say, father unknown. Afterward the child would google his mother's name and get 224,000 hits.

Once in a while everyone wishes someone dead, though no one should ever kill. It's human to consider it sometimes. People who drive recklessly in densely settled areas close to schools and kindergartens. Threats issued in dark alleys generally license killing, in the same way as unlawful confinement or being a soldier at war. Marginalization is no excuse, and neither is seeing a woman in the supermarket at closing time putting groceries into the shopping cart of a man like the one he remembers from childhood who used to play the banjo at get-togethers in the community hall. Balding and flabby, with thin arms and a yearning to be possessed by something big. The kind of person you feel for, the way you feel for horses and cows whose hind legs are going lame and who are unaware that the faint sound of metal on metal in the darkness of the shed is the sound of cartridges being loaded into a gun. Kill or be killed. Thoughts like that are free. Fun, even. Though not for Aileen Wuornos's biological child. Not with 224,000 hits for his mother's name on Google.

He looks at his hands. His right hand is on the mouse, and when he switches off the computer in just a moment he knows he'll feel like he did when he used to look at *Playboy*. Even after the magazine was hidden away he could still sense the sweet smell of spit on the glossy page. And yet he keeps clicking, to Dagmar Overbye. It's what he wants right now: to vanish into her tiny rooms on the web, and she is dark, full, and rather out of focus, like something from a fairy tale. It's

hard to relate to her having been a real person, though she was. Sentenced to death for eight of the twenty-five infant killings she is thought to have committed. They called her the Angel Maker, and it's the way she did it that puzzles him. She put a notice in the paper for young women in unfortunate circumstances and promised to discreetly arrange adoption for a fee. But when she got the money and the young mother had gone, Dagmar, out of her mind on naphtha and ether, did away with the child. She put one of them in the toilet, another she wrapped up in newspapers, then took her daughter by the hand and went out to bury it. During the trial it came out that as they were walking the bundle slipped from Dagmar's hands: Mother dropped her parcel, said the daughter, and it's impossible to imagine what it must have been like to have such a mother.

He remembers his own as a dry rustling sound, always bent over work: a kneading board, trays of bread buns, minced pork, layer cakes, and See how he runs! And when he thinks of her it's by the cherry tree in the front garden.

But Dagmar is in fog, a bitter cold morning in Copenhagen, and she is standing still in a black dress with puffed sleeves and laced boots. She has a parcel under her arm, wrapped in newspaper, and that's what seeps in and out of his chest. The parcel, and the thought of the twenty-five small bodies she concealed in attics or burned in the stove, and the fact she was never able to explain why she did it. She was out of her mind on naphtha, she said. It was like being in a dream that couldn't be described.

He knows it's hard for normal people to understand the part that couldn't be described. Dagmar Overbye wasn't normal,

but when he did his military service they said women could be good and efficient fighters. They could even be vicious. All they needed was to cross over a line, the sergeant said. Once they'd crossed it they had no problem with killing. Personally he has no wish to know what line that is, but something tells him that in the cases of Dagmar and Aileen there must have been some foregoing demoralization. Damage set off by comfortless upbringing, perhaps even a kind of mental illness. It would explain a lot, if that were the case. It would make things understandable. Anomaly is within the bounds. The abnormal can be accepted, it can even open doors in a person and make room for everyone to be human, he thinks. But then it might be something else altogether. Something more frightening.

He remembers a night not long ago when he stayed up after the retiree had logged off. That night he read online in the tabloid that chimpanzees were able to make spears for hunting. A team of scientists in the West African state of Senegal had observed behavioral changes in apes in an area without food. He read how they noticed the apes began to hunt with spears. That was one thing, but only the young apes and the females did so. The old males sat around and starved, the article said. They weren't good at thinking new thoughts, a female scientist commented. She talked about how with her own eyes she had seen a female chimp spear one of the monkeys the locals called bush babies. This particular bush baby lay sleeping in its den, and the scientist described how the chimp used the spear to prod the monkey out of the den and then killed it and ate it. That same night he googled *bush baby* and the screen filled up with pictures. They had big, black, bulging eyes and were by nature clearly terrified, like Dagmar's twenty-five infants or

Aileen Wuornos's biological child just after reading the first article about his mother. That's what the bush babies looked like, paralyzed with fear, and yet the old males just sat around waiting to be possessed by something big. A savannah full of males with banjos, he thought, and females with hair under their arms. And spears.

He switches off the computer and turns on the desk lamp. He sits still with his hands on his knees until the hard drive has stopped whirring. They make up all sorts of things, he thinks to himself. Then he takes off his shoes so as not to make a noise when he goes up the stairs to her.

# FLIGHT

IT'S A YEAR NOW SINCE ALLAN MOVED OUT, AND WE had no children, though both us were able. He once told me I was like the castles he used to build out of straw bales when he was a boy. Inside the castle was a den in which to eat cookies and drink fruit juice while listening to the rumble of the combine in the next field. That's what being with me was like, Allan said. Another time he said I reminded him of a doghouse his father had. As a boy, he used to sit inside the doghouse with the German wirehaired pointer. It was cozy, and sometimes he would think of what it would be like if a girl suddenly crawled in to be with him. That was me, and he meant it nicely.

Allan worked for Vestas and traveled to wind farms abroad as a consultant and service technician. When he came home he found it hard to explain to me what he had seen and done. He spoke of great landscapes, bigger than anything a person could imagine, and I would nod, which annoyed him. For Christmas one year I bought him a digital camera so he could e-mail me photos when he was traveling. That way we could better share his experiences, so I thought. I still have pictures on my computer of Allan in front of various foreign attractions. One of the pictures I don't know what to do with shows Allan next to a wind turbine that's still laid out on the ground. Behind him is a vista of pine trees and rocks fading away into

what looks like infinity. The picture is from Dolly Sods, West Virginia, and when he got back he was quiet.

I don't know how long he brooded, but one evening after we had eaten he said it was okay if I kept the house, but he needed to move out. There was nothing wrong with me, he said, he just felt like he was in a vacuum. He took two suitcases and filled them with clothes. He took the dog, too, and said he would drive over to his parents'. I realized he didn't mean for it to be a break but something final, and yet I still went outside with him and waved as he backed out of the driveway. I particularly remember the front door when I turned to go back inside. The light from the lamp shining on the wall cladding and door handle. That sort of thing.

In the days after he moved out I didn't know what to do with myself. Whenever my mother called, I didn't tell her he was gone and answered her questions about the things we were doing. In order not to go into what had happened, I let her do most of the talking while I looked out the window at the hedge. It won't grow, and I've planted bulbs all along its length to make up for it, but there's no joy from bulbs in November.

I spent time waiting for the reaction, only it didn't come, and time passed best when I sat at the computer. Finding information about places like Dolly Sods is easy on the Internet, and I could see how vast and beautiful and desolate it was. In Dolly Sods, there are places where no one has even been yet. Distances and depths of that magnitude are amazing, and I imagined how Allan had stood there with his hand on the wind turbine. I didn't cry. Not even when I finally told my mother and father. I explained to them it was for the best, and I made it sound like I'd been involved in the decision.

My mother was disappointed, though she found it commendable that I'd taken it so well. It was true. My colleagues said so too, they praised me for dealing with it so well. Allan was also impressed, and we soon found a friendly tone, especially when he phoned. We could even laugh, and I could hear his voice relax at the other end. About three months after he moved out, he called one evening and said he was being sent to Turkey. He was going to install new turbines on a plateau there. How exciting, I said. And he said: Yes, I'm looking forward to it. There was a silence, and then he said he was very happy and grateful to me for taking it all so well.

Afterward, I sat in the kitchen. I looked at the bulletin board and the magnets on the refrigerator. I brewed coffee and watched the water as it ran through. I sat down at the counter again. When I drank the coffee, I felt something go wrong inside me. It was as if it tasted too big, and the same with the soda, the licorice, the maple syrup, and the Greek yogurt I ate later on. I was agitated, restless, and the only thing that helped was to chew on something. But it was never sufficient. Every time I ate something I would have to put something else in my mouth. I couldn't stop, and the night didn't help. I walked through the house thinking of grapes, and I've never been the kind of person who could eat whatever I wanted. At two in the morning I thought fresh air might do the trick. I stood out back and looked out over the landscape. I could see the stream winding through the meadow. There was frost in the grass, and then I began to cry.

It came from way down, from a place I didn't think I had, and it hurt, too. To make it keep on hurting, I imagined I ate up all the grass, all the cows, all the birds. I pictured myself

stuffing the meadow, the stream, its banks, and soil into my mouth. I forced all kinds of things into my stomach: church steeples, castles made of straw bales, silos. The grove on the other side of the stream, and the military training area behind the barracks. Eventually, all that was left was me and the tuft of grass on which I balanced. That, and a great NM72C wind turbine I refused to devour. And since you can't eat yourself, I went home.

The next morning was Sunday and I drove over to my parents'. I had bread rolls and pastries with me, and the carrier bag full of magazines I'd borrowed from my mother. She could tell by looking at me that I hadn't slept well, but she didn't delve. We talked about my sister's husband and their kids instead. We talked about my brother's wife, because no one gets on with her. And we talked about Allan, too, because he wasn't like that at all. They liked Allan, and it all would have turned out differently if we'd ever had kids. I said he was going to Turkey to work for a while. My mother said she didn't understand why he always had to be on the move. I nodded, and my father found an ad in the paper he wanted me to see.

When I was sixteen, I told my mother I wasn't sure I wanted to have children when I was old enough. There were other things in life than kids, I said. My mother ought to know, because my aunt once said Mom cried when she found out she was going to have me. But she has a habit of forgetting things that don't suit her, and she was pleased when I came home and said I'd met Allan. It's always been hard to find gifts for my mother, but when someone gives her something she never has the heart to throw it away again. The attic is full of old newspapers, worn-out clothes in trash bags, furniture, cheap

novels, souvenirs, knitting, and potted plants put away for the winter. When I was a child, I was certain that if there was ever any danger I would hide in the attic. Nothing could get to me there. I would take the rugs down from the beams to make a den. I would have freezer bags full of soft cookies. Fruit juice in water bottles with screw caps that smelled of mold. From below would be the sound of the transistor radio that kept losing its frequency and had to be retuned all the time, and I would see myself running bare-legged through the paddock, not caring about stepping in the cowpats, not caring about touching the wire at the end and getting an electric shock, but running all the way down to the stream and leaping across, and I could feel it still as we sat there and drank our coffee: the feeling of taking flight.

"There are other men," Mom said all of a sudden, and smiled at me over her pastry.

"I suppose," I said, and then Dad handed me the coffee pot.

My head was empty as I drove home and I felt like crying again. I tried to set myself off by thinking of various things, but couldn't. I even thought of Dolly Sods in West Virginia, and the wind turbine that was yet to be erected. It didn't help, and Dolly Sods simply made me put my foot down even harder on the gas pedal. Dolly Sods is mostly a wilderness from which vast amounts of water run into the Mississippi River that flows through the middle of the United States and divides it in two. That's what I thought to myself as I drove through the hills. Dolly Sods is huge, and not many years ago no one lived there at all. The people who lived on its edge were scared. For them, it was an ominous place, full of wild animals and deep abysses. There were stories of hunters venturing too far into

Dolly Sods and never being seen again. When I got home I sat in the car outside. I thought about going away. I could still do what I wanted. I didn't need to ask permission of anyone. I could go to the United States and rent a car as simple as that. I could drive straight to Dolly Sods and park the car on its perimeter. I could put my camera on the hood and photograph myself there, in walking boots, a white T-shirt, and sunglasses, looking just like other people in photos.

I pulled the key from the ignition and leaned back against the headrest. I told myself I would do just that. I sat there and looked in the side mirror, and promised myself I'd think about it.

# NAT NEWSOM

IF I WERE TO SINGLE OUT ONE PERSON IN PARTICULAR from my extensive studies of human behavior it would have to be Nat Newsom, whom I knew ten years ago, or rather ran into outside the McDonald's I passed each day on my way to work at Columbia University. Nat Newsom opened the door for the customers of McDonald's while rattling a plastic cup he for want of a better solution had taped to his wrist. The reason Nat more than anyone else stands out for me as special is not simply that he was able to keep his spirits up despite lacking health care and the deposit his former landlord had vanished into thin air with. That was part of it, but more specifically it was because of the paradox of Nat, *genetically predisposed to naïveté* as he was, lacking the very quality that characterizes the condition.

A person is born with the ability to reach out for things in the world. Thus, an infant will clutch at any finger that is extended toward it, for the child wants to live, and in order to live it must get its hands dirty. It is the retention of this basic reaching out into the world that characterizes genetic predisposition to naïveté in the adult human. It's bred into us. The monkey's young reach immediately for the mother's fur and use its tufts as handles during transport on their perilous way through the jungle, and on another level we must not forget

that the reflex moreover is cosmic, since humans reach out in more or less the same way to God and all else unknown. But let's return to Nat Newsom.

Nat Newsom stood outside McDonald's every day trying to make it look like he was helping people by opening and closing the door. The reality of the matter was that his handicap prevented him from truly making a difference, but at least he showed himself to be willing. Doing so allowed him to save up so that at the end of the day he could go through the door himself and purchase a Happy Meal. Having observed Nat Newsom for some time, I decided one morning to ask if he would be interested in taking part in my study of existential behavior at Columbia's philosophy department, where I am known as Professor Jack Soya. Nat agreed, and we arranged to meet over a beer in a bar that same evening. Nat showed up on time.

He told me he was born to an alcoholic mother who had also experimented with amphetamines during the pregnancy, a cocktail that resulted in Nat entering the world as smooth as soap, unable to grasp hold of anything at all. Where his fingers were supposed to be he had only stumps, so Nat drank his beer through a straw. I studied his hands as he did so: both were equipped with a minuscule thumb that more than anything else resembled a baby kangaroo when, tiny and covered in slime, it slips out of the female kangaroo's birth canal to slowly (and, in accordance with its genetic predisposition, naïvely) crawl upward through its mother's fur and into her pouch, there to latch onto the nipple with its entire body, which mostly consists of a mouth. A journey, incidentally, that may be compared to the (likewise innately naïve) wandering made

by the newly hatched young of the sea turtle amid a rain of dive-bombing seagulls from their warm hollow in the sand to the infinitely large and embracing ocean.

Nat Newsom grew up without the ability to think strategically, yet with an abundance of enterprise and a close relationship to his mother's sister, who quickly took her place. *My aunt could not be brought down,* Nat told me, and I dwelled on his comment. People like Nat Newsom appear to be equipped with their own center of gravity insofar as they seem able to maintain an open outlook on the world almost regardless of whatever it may allot them. This is not to say that this naïveté cannot take up temporary residence in the prison of the mind if, during an attempt to reach out, it happens to burn its fingers. But inside, such people are toddlers. They look at their burns and bruises, their emptied bank accounts and broken dreams, as though it were an eternal source of astonishment to them that malice actually exists.

I would like to stress this propensity to wonder, this willingness to believe, by relating one key scene in Nat Newsom's life. One day in front of the New York Public Library, Nat and a friend are accosted by a man wearing a cheap suit. The man in question is white, a matter of no real consequence, but on the lapel of his jacket is affixed an ID badge with a black man's photograph on it. The badge says the man's name is Charlie, and yet this white man introduces himself as Kevin Miller. Charlie or Kevin addresses Nat Newsom's buddy, not Nat himself, who is visibly handicapped. The man stands right up close to Nat's buddy and says he can see he pumps iron. And then he produces a questionnaire and a ballpoint pen from a pocket of his suit.

From the sideline Nat now witnesses this man with the two names explain to his friend that he is from a university up in Harlem. He tells him he is collecting money for a rehab program for drug addicts. He wants to know if Nat's buddy would like to make a donation, and he would also like to know what gym he goes to. Nat Newsom's buddy is not a homosexual, and yet Nat can tell he is flattered when the man says that *he* is, and that he likes men with the build of Nat's buddy.

Two things are happening here. One is that Nat's buddy is disarmed by charm. The hustler, which of course is what the man is, caresses the buddy's ego, which according to Nat Newsom was an easy target for flattery. The fact that Nat's friend gets taken for a ride is due to this flaw in his personality and not to his being genetically predisposed to naïveté. And we should believe Nat, for whom lying was so difficult, when he claims that his buddy was not in the slightest bit naïve. But Nat, who *was* predisposed in that way, catches on to the nature of the transaction. What happens with Nat is that one part of him thinks: *What a nice guy, and it's such a good thing there are people willing to help drug addicts,* while another part thinks: *This guy is a swindler, cheating unsuspecting people out of their money.* Nat Newsom is of two minds. He can see that the questionnaire doesn't even mention drug addicts. He can see that the black man is white. Nothing adds up, but despite this double insight Nat neglects to warn his buddy. Moreover, he does nothing to stop him handing over ten dollars for the rehab program in Harlem. And not only that: Nat Newsom turns his backside to the swindler and asks him to take ten dollars out of his back pocket. *I can't do it myself,* says Nat,

waving his little thumbs and stumps in front of the guy, who gladly helps him out with his problem.

As we sat there in the bar I asked Nat Newsom why he hadn't intervened to stop the hustle. I asked him, too, why he let himself be shaken down like that. I recall Nat's tiny thumbs on the tabletop as he sucked his beer through his straw. Then he leaned back and explained to me that if the world was like a person sometimes thought it was, then he wouldn't have the courage to even open his eyes in the mornings. He also said that if it was a choice between losing ten dollars and losing confidence in the possibility of people being called Kevin and Charlie and being black and white at the same time, then he preferred to lose ten dollars.

I never made use of Nat Newsom in my studies of genetically predisposed naïveté. He was too odd for that. But even though as research material he was unsuitable for my dissertation, *Jack Soya's Laws of Strategy,* I will never forget him, not least because a short time later someone kicked him so hard in the head during an incident out at JFK that what little sense he had inside him could not be saved. I briefly considered adding him to the notes, but decided against it. A good scientist is known by his ability to select.

# HAIR SALON

I LIVE IN A TWO-ROOM APARTMENT IN A BUILDING away from the center. It's not long since I moved out here and I don't know many people. I asked the hairstylist on the opposite corner how much he charged compared to the ones in the city:

"Practically nothing," he said, and asked me to lean my head back farther.

For smoking cigarettes and drinking coffee with the hairstylist I get my hair done for half price. Once in a while, the fat lady who lives in our building walks by on the street outside. She has permission to keep a dog in her apartment, because her dog can't bark. I asked the hairstylist what kind of a dog can't bark. He said it was because the fat lady gives the dog her medication. Apparently, she said it's to be on the safe side. Which is fine by me. I don't care one way or the other, and when the hairstylist asks me why I'm down in the dumps I talk about something else, or I say with a wry smile I don't like to see in the mirror:

"Oh, the usual stuff."

That makes him think it's to do with men, and he can think what he wants. I can see the fat lady from my building tying up her dog outside the Laundromat across the street. We usually say hello, and I think it's because she once helped

me out in the Laundromat. I've often seen her on the bench in the park, sharing a beer with one of the locals. She's always doing something, and now she goes inside the Laundromat as the hairstylist sprays my hair. He says I have split ends and wants to sell me silk oil from America, but I'm not buying any.

"It's all about loving yourself. If you don't love yourself, who else will?" the hairstylist says.

Someone, I think to myself, and gaze out at the fat lady's dog. It's sitting nicely outside the Laundromat. It's turned to face the corner of the building, though not as if waiting for something to appear. It's a nice dog. I've seen it often, of course, plodding along at its mom's heel, but I never noticed what it actually looked like before.

"I wonder if it knows it's out of its skull," I say to the hairstylist, and he tells me it's a cairn terrier.

"Well, it's out of its skull, anyway," I say.

We talk about what she gives it. The hairstylist thinks it might be diet pills. I say pancakes and estrogen. We laugh, and then the hairstylist says they've raised their prices at the Laundromat. Now it costs twenty-three kroner for seven kilos, thirty-eight for more. He thinks it's extortion, but I don't care. I never have more than seven kilos of laundry and have reached the point where I never will, unless I start stealing things. I say that to the hairstylist and we laugh about it, though I don't care to see myself laughing in the mirror. It looks like I have no teeth.

It was at the Laundromat I met the fat lady the first time. She showed me how the soap dispenser worked and where the little cups were for the softener. She was doing laundry for someone else, she said, and didn't think she'd seen me before

in the neighborhood. I said I'd just moved here from the center and she nodded slightly.

When I came to get my laundry out of the washing machine she was still there. I had some trouble with the spinner and she's the type who wants to help. She took control of my laundry. She rolled the trolley with my laundry over to the spinner and put my underwear inside piece by piece. She asked what number I lived at, and it turned out she went to the residents' bingo nights with someone who lived on the first floor. While she was telling me about all the things she had won over the years, I was thinking she must have been young in the seventies. She was probably a bit chubby, but pretty. She'd have worn white jeans with bell-bottoms. She'd have had blouses with puffed sleeves, and her hair would have been fair and turned with a curling iron. Good company, but at some point she decided it was better to love everyone than just someone, and after that she just got bigger.

"All it needs is a quick spin," she said, and I didn't care that she'd had her hands in my underwear.

"Thanks for the help," I said. "Anytime," she said.

Now she thinks she knows me. If she's out with the dog, she waves, and if she's standing in one of the other lines at the supermarket, she'll call out:

"Hey, how are you doing?"

"Fine!" I call back, and I don't even know her name.

Sometimes she'll come up to me on the sidewalk and tell me something trivial. One day, for instance, she stopped me to say someone new had moved into the apartment above her and that the person in question was noisy. The neighbors on her left always had their windows open to the courtyard, so

all their conversations echoed in her kitchen, and the ones on her right were always doing it, as she put it. Morning, noon, and night they were doing it, she said, then made moaning noises and funny faces to avoid having to say sex, and she must have had the dog with her that day. I don't know why I never really looked at it before. Its coat is brown, though graying at the ends. It wears a red collar.

"How about a smoke?" the hairstylist says, and I nod.

He goes into the little kitchen out back to get a pack of cigarettes and an ashtray. He has put his things, scissors and oil, on the counter in front of me, and while he's away the fat lady comes out of the Laundromat across the street. I've seen her a couple of times standing in the store picking out pastries with another fat lady. She waves to me. I stick my hand out from under the cape and wave back. I think the hairstylist may be right, that it's some kind of terrier. I can see her talking to it as they go down the street together. Valium, I think to myself, and the sun beats down on the pavement.

# THE HERON

I WON'T FEED BIRDS, BUT IF YOU MUST, THEN YOU should do so in Frederiksberg Gardens. There are tame herons in Frederiksberg Gardens, and the park authorities have placed the park's benches at some distance from one another so as not to attract too many birds to one area. There are problems at the end of the park where the alcoholics sit, particularly with ducks, but I never go that way, and you can see the herons everywhere. Of the heron itself, one can only say that from a distance it looks impressive, but this doesn't apply when you get close up. It's too thin, and tame herons in particular look malnourished. Most likely all that bread gives the herons of Frederiksberg Gardens bad stomachs and is to blame for their not making an effort to fly. Last winter I saw one slouching on the back of a bench with its long, scrawny neck. Its feet were completely white and it barely even reacted when I walked past. The way the wind ruffled its neck feathers made me want to go back and sit down next to it. It was the way the suffering had to be drawn out like that, the way herons never really muster the enthusiasm. But I won't touch birds, alive or dead. They shouldn't be played with, and you should take care never to touch other people with your infected hands. If a bird is dead make sure not to come into contact either with it or with its excrement. Disposable gloves must be used, and

the bird should be picked up with a plastic bag, the way you pick up dog shit. The bag should be sealed and disposed of with the household garbage or else buried. How difficult is that, with all the knowledge we have available?

In order to avoid herons in large numbers, as well as the strange man who often stands on the path leading to the Chinese Pavilion and feeds them herrings while claiming to be able to talk to them, I tend to walk instead around Damhus Pond. At Damhus Pond whatever a heron might have to say is meaningless. Besides, herons have difficulty colonizing Damhus Pond because of the nearby houses, the foot traffic, and all the cyclists. It's easy to see from the detritus littering the water's edge that the pond has been ruined by cyclists. There are many out-of-place objects there, and as well as bikes they once found a dismembered female body in a suitcase in the pond. An entire woman in little pieces put into freezer bags. The suitcase was found by someone out walking his dog. Or, presumably, it was the dog that found it. Credit where it's due. There are always lots of dogs around Damhus Pond, and I can picture this particular dog very clearly as I walk along the path. It's a golden retriever and it's fussing in front of the suitcase, which has drifted halfway up onto the shore. The golden retriever has a secret urge to roll around in carcasses, preferably those of birds or mice, but how is it to tell the difference? I can picture it, and I can imagine its owner at the moment the realization kicks in. I imagine he remembers the moment the suitcase was opened whenever he is getting ready to take a trip, and likely even the dog was never the same again.

Things are contagious. Things want to get in through the cracks. That's the way they are, and I know from a former

colleague of mine that the woman was killed and dismembered in an apartment in the Vesterbro district and that the girl who lived in the apartment downstairs and who was studying veterinary science moved out not long afterward, even though her upstairs neighbor had been apprehended and sentenced for the murder. Who could blame her? She probably kept thinking about all the times she had passed him on the stairs. Most likely she felt the building was contaminated and even the slightest sound reminded her of the night she heard something going on upstairs. But something is always going on in the night, there are always smells and sounds: pigeons rustling in the attic, creatures on the move, and the herons of Frederiksberg Gardens can sometimes be seen, looking like gray poultry shears in the sky over Valby. The heron is an awkward bird in flight, and the Heron Man on the path leading to the Chinese Pavilion would do well to tell the herons so, seeing as how he's always babbling away at them like that.

Although my apartment is on Frederiksberg Avenue I willingly walk the extra distance to Damhus Pond to escape the gathering of birds, and as for dismembered bodies I've walked around the pond most of my life without ever finding one myself. When I was a child, my friends and I would run around the pond because our physical-education teachers at Vigerslev Allé School told us to do so. I still see children who look like me and my best friend, the dentist's son, Lorenz, running around the pond. Whenever a tall, skinny boy runs past me, I picture Lorenz racing to come in first. I tend to stop and smile when I see kids running around the pond like that. But after going around it myself I no longer want to stop and smile at anyone, certainly not the young women

with their stony faces and big baby carriages. They always come in flocks, great flocks of mothers, and they stir up bad feelings in one another, so none of them will even look at you when you walk past.

I step aside into the grass, thinking about the dog, the suitcase, the body, and how the veterinary student lost her swagger overnight, and how it doesn't take a doctorate to have kids. I have known hopeless individuals to have children. It doesn't require much more than a certain degree of sexual excitement, at least in the male, and at any rate it's not the women with the baby carriages who are in charge of the biology of it. If anyone is in charge of the biology it's God, but they probably made Him step aside, too. No one at the age of those mothers believes she needs eternal life, and even the concept of giving way to oncoming traffic seems unreasonable. But it's important to me, and sometimes when those mothers have passed by I look back at them and wonder what it would be like if they swelled up. They'd begin to expand, and eventually they'd expand so much that they could no longer keep themselves together, and then I picture them exploding: shreds of flesh in the trees and along the shore, blood spattering on the swans, the ducks, and the coots floundering in the grass. There's a rustling in the grass, the kind that makes dogs want to roll on the banks. I hear the rustle, and I hear the babies screaming in their carriages. I picture Lorenz skating through the mud, racing on around the pond on his pale, thin legs, long since dead, eaten up from within by sick-cell divisions, cremated and interred into the ground, while I keep walking, through the dead birds and the dead mothers, to get to the baby carriages. I have to be careful not to lose my balance, and then I reach

my hand down into one of the baby carriages left behind, my hand with a cookie in it, and the child inside looks up at me with eyes full of astonishment. I pick it up. I lift it high into the air, and the movement causes its pacifier and its rattle to fall to the ground. I wish the child no harm; all I want is to lift it into the air before putting it back and walking home through Frederiksberg Gardens.

The heron was there last winter. Sitting with its beard blowing in the wind and its long pale toes clutching the back of the bench. Incapable of fright, tired and sallow in its gaze, smelling of the mites that lived in its underfeathers, and I should have sat down next to it.

# KARATE CHOP

SHE HAD ONCE BEEN ADVISED TO LISTEN CLOSELY TO what a man said just when he began to sense a woman was showing interest in him. For unknown reasons, most men at that very moment give off important information about their true nature. This was what she had been told, and she had known men herself who, in the middle of an intimate conversation on a very different subject altogether, could say:

"You should know I'm not an easy man to live with."

Or: "I can be such an asshole at times."

Mostly, she had considered this to be self-deprecation, if not a form of politeness, and if she did not take it seriously it was because she had not understood that a person could be in possession of disturbing knowledge about himself and still have no wish to change. For that reason, and because she lived for the idea that everything had some deeper reason, she never believed what these men said about themselves. It was hard for her to acknowledge that their words really were intended to be warnings and that her failure to listen would end up costing her dearly, but she went so far as to agree with them when afterward they said:

"It wasn't like you didn't know or anything. I told you how I was."

And indeed they had, yet still the problem recurred with

the next one, and the next one again, and every time the man sensed she was about to make herself vulnerable to him, he told her something disturbing about himself. Annelise would smile then and say:

"Oh, stop it."

But they never did.

When she met Carl Erik Juhl, what made her fall for him, in effect, was his long list of disturbing traits. Working with children with psychological problems and learning difficulties, she was used to meeting adults who were disinclined to acknowledge their own weaknesses, and in that respect Carl Erik's frankness seemed redeeming. He had been called in for a meeting at the school about her sessions with his son, Kasper, who was in seventh grade, and almost at the very instant he stepped inside her office Carl Erik confessed that he had a temper, was something of a coward and a poor father to boot. Annelise pushed back her chair slightly so as to get a better look at him. And there he was. His face was round, his hair thin and curly. He looked out the window behind her, and his smile was so sweet her heart turned somersaults.

What she wondered now was whom to blame for the wounds her relationship with Carl Erik Juhl had inflicted upon her. She turned her body in front of the mirror in the bedroom and lifted her right arm, on which was a bruise. It was quite unacceptable of him, yet at the same time her not listening to what he told her was suspicious. Not one of the traits he had ascribed to himself that day in her office had he failed to demonstrate in practice.

She sat down at an angle on the edge of the bed and frowned. There had to be a reason, and one had first to look

to oneself to discover what was wrong. Her upbringing had been decent enough, though one time when she was about ten and had fallen off her bike and ended up in the hospital, her father had not even come to visit. Not caring for the smell of hospitals, he had stayed home instead. It was by no means unlikely that some encoding of basic insignificance and a tendency to neglect one's own needs had taken place then and left its mark. Or perhaps it was her relationship with her brother. Arne had been good at sports and wouldn't bother playing with her unless she was able to take the ball from him at soccer. Their mother had always been so quiet, too, and yet to no avail, Annelise thought to herself and pulled the comforter up over her shoulders. Judging from the students she treated, not many children escaped a beating of one sort or another. But that didn't necessarily turn them into thugs, masochists, and murderers. There had to be more basic psychological traits, perhaps even gender related, that could account for her behavior. Carl Erik's too, for that matter. He was always falling short, and she could never make an issue big enough. It was no good.

Annelise gazed down perplexed at her right hand, and as she did so she thought about how, when they had started going out together, Carl Erik liked when she was drunk. He wanted her with him out on the town and encouraged her to flirt.

"There's no one in here you couldn't have," he'd say, looking proudly around the bar.

On occasion he picked out some poor guy, preferably with a slight handicap if anyone like that was around, and when Annelise came back from the bathroom he would bundle her onto a bar stool next to the victim and whisper:

"This one's down on his luck. Show him a good time, it'll cheer him up."

She would dance with this other man, or allow him to buy her a beer. She had thought of it as Carl Erik's way of paying her a compliment. Now it was obvious to her that it was something else altogether. There must be a hundred ways of rolling out the red carpet in front of an ailing store, Annelise thought. Giving a woman away to a cripple is only one of them.

But she had known many men like that. Many men like those reptiles in the zoo that could puff up their faces with fanciful color and raise themselves up onto thin toes and rattle. Every woman in the world would meet one sooner or later. It was all part and parcel. But she was no good at not loving them, even if there were no obvious reason to do so.

She looked into the mirror again and let the comforter slip down her shoulders. She saw how her breasts and hair hung limply from her body. She saw a red mark beneath her collarbone, and maybe the problem was at root sexual. Maybe she just didn't understand how to deal with male sexuality. As a child, Arne had kept porn magazines under his mattress. Sometimes when he was out at soccer practice she lifted the mattress and flicked through them. As she gazed at the glitzy images, feeling a tingle inside, she thought a woman would have to love a man very much to put that thing into her mouth, and she thought too that the man would have to love it very much to want to put it inside the woman's mouth. She found the anal business odd. There was something anatomical about it she still had not fully understood. In her view it was about little more than the instrumental power of the male organ. Because it could be inserted into openings, it had to be inserted

into openings. In her hometown there was a man who went around sticking his thing through gaps in fences and the wire baskets on bicycles. Instrumental power, she thought to herself. Technical pleasure ought never to be underestimated as an element of male sexuality, and it wasn't that she disliked sex, it just wasn't all kinds of sex she liked, and she could still feel Carl Erik inside her.

Now he lay naked under the comforter and they would never go to bed together again. Never, for now she hurt all over and was unable to see what she had done wrong. But what had happened was that Carl Erik's son Kasper had been staying with him that weekend. Things had not gone well, she sensed when Carl Erik had come over just before dinner. Kasper had said something about the sessions Annelise had been having with him, but first she and Carl Erik had eaten dinner and shared a bottle of wine, and then they had fucked, drunk more wine, and taken a shower, and it was all fine until she made to dry Carl Erik's back. That was when he became annoyed about her having to touch everything and not leave things alone, always poking and meddling and sticking her nose into the slightest thing. It was as though she were never satisfied with the knowledge she had, he yelled at her, and the last thing she remembered before he blew up at her was the sentence *All that crap you've been telling Kasper, for instance.* And at that point she had asked for the crap to be expounded upon, which was what then happened in the hallway, the living room, the kitchen, and the bedroom.

She was perfectly willing to admit that she had lost confidence in her choices. She kept on mostly because she was scared of giving up on her urge to be happy and simply content

herself with peace and quiet. Sitting there on the edge of the bed, she considered that she had most likely seen her worst and her best now. She had been down on all fours, on the edge of her nerves, naked and bound and temporarily insane at the time of the crime.

She climbed gingerly back into bed. There was Carl Erik, unconcerned by her still being awake. His hand was next to her face, clutching at a corner of the comforter. It looked gentle lying there. A little red across the knuckles, but there was nothing wrong with its outline, especially not if Annelise put her eyes slightly out of focus. She considered its shape and thought about the lines; everything you wanted to see but which in actual fact was not there. Everything that should have been but which never became, and this was important to understand. Not only in respect to herself. It was something she could put to use with the children at school. She recalled that as a child she had been heavily seduced by the black line drawings in coloring books. They were done so well she always wanted to fill in the empty spaces with crayon and felt-tip. Behind that burning desire to color in the drawings lay the creative human's longing to give life, and, not least: to make the drawings her own. In a way, it was like stealing preconceived ideas. The drawing could never be lifelike, and for that reason you reached a point where you began to draw outside the lines.

She had observed that children only seldom showed the colored-in drawings in their coloring books to their parents or other adults. Presumably because they were such poor indicators of the child's creative abilities and demonstrated all too clearly their less flattering traits: laziness and lack of confidence

to really get below the surface of things. Annelise's gaze fell once more upon Carl Erik. One of his kind—a man—was part of the idea preconceived for women. More than that, any individual you happened to meet was nothing but a potential, an outline to be colored in and assigned content. She had read about it in respect to young girls and their propensity to overfunction—the need to change, control, expound upon. But you can't do that, and eventually you pick up the felt-tip with the most in it and color everything in. Maybe that was why he hit her? Maybe her bruises were just a way of coloring outside the lines? Maybe the reason he turned her onto her stomach, pressed her into the mattress, and fucked her from behind as she sobbed and felt her legs grow heavy was to make her real and living by being careless, and seen from the opposite viewpoint what she did afterward while he was asleep was the same, outside the lines, outside them all, even if the result as it lay there in a mess of blood and comforter seemed to be anything else but alive.

# MOTHER, GRANDMOTHER, AND AUNT ELLEN

HE REMEMBERS HIS GRANDMOTHER, BUT EVERYTHING that happened before he was born comes from his mother and Aunt Ellen. They were full of stories, and right from the beginning they wanted to tell them all, and when they did they would look at him as if to encourage him to learn them by heart. Aunt Ellen, for instance, told how one time toward the end of the war they were baking vanilla cookies, but then the mailman came. As he turned into the farmyard, Grandmother got down on the floor and began to scrub the linoleum with her ass in the air. Grandfather was sitting in the parlor studying aerial photos of Leipzig and his mother had gone out to the rabbits in the cowshed. It was nearly Christmas and the mailman winked at Aunt Ellen and said something about the vanilla cookies smelling good. Grandmother sat like a mermaid on the floor and said with a giggle that she couldn't get up again. The mailman had to help her while Ellen tried to close the door into the parlor with cookie dough on her hands.

But what bothered Aunt Ellen was afterward when the mailman had gone and Grandfather went out to the rabbits.

Grandmother had that look on her face. She stood at the kitchen sink with one of Aunt Ellen's vanilla cookies in her mouth and said it had no taste.

"She could be like that," Aunt Ellen had said so often, and he doesn't know how many times he saw his mother nod and put in her two cents. "You remember what she was like, don't you?" they would say, and scrutinize him.

He remembers his grandmother well. She was small, almost like a child, though very round. She had five children, and her sons left home as soon as they could. He doesn't remember Grandfather, and to him Grandmother was a woman who lived in an apartment building in town and grew increasingly odd, while Aunt Ellen and his mother took turns making dinner for her. Certain smells made him think of her, smells that linger in the bathroom, or bergamot candy in the kitchen. Or the sight of dish mats and the plastic souvenirs his mother and Aunt Ellen brought home from vacations. And her hands, mostly her hands. They were as small as a little girl's and never at rest. Small and fluttering. How strange to think it was those hands that did it. The thing his mother claimed they did.

Another story they liked to tell was about the last years of the war when the tethered cow had to be moved. His mother loved it when Aunt Ellen told the story. She would light up a cigarette and sit nodding with it. It happened when the Allies attacked the landing strip and the Germans retaliated. Grandmother was afraid the cow tied up in the meadow would be killed. So Aunt Ellen had to go and move it. Of course, she was afraid, but Grandmother insisted the cow be brought to safety. Naturally, the animal was terrified, so it galloped around with Aunt Ellen hanging on to the rope behind it. The planes

were diving in over the trees and the southern end of the potato field. Grandmother crawled on all fours to the gable end of the house to find shelter from the shrapnel.

"There she was with her ass in the air barking out instructions about which way I should run."

That's how Aunt Ellen told the story, and then she would grimace and stress that the secret to understanding Grandmother was that she wasn't very intelligent. She was stupid, Aunt Ellen would say, and his mother would snigger and Aunt Ellen would look at her sister with a flicker in her eye.

"That's the way she was. Mother was stupid."

It always went quiet between them then. Aunt Ellen would change the subject, or decide it was time to go home. She lived in the building opposite and the last thing he and his mother always did before they went to bed was stand at the window of the living room and wave to her.

All the time his mother lay sick, she and Ellen never spoke of Grandmother and her ways. But then his mother died, and after the funeral the subject came up between him and Aunt Ellen. It was his initiative. He took his aunt to a cafeteria and asked her about the old days. He assumed it was for want of anything better, but she told the story about the cow and the air raid once again.

"She was so stupid," said Aunt Ellen, and he could see it was like the bottom fell out of her because his mother no longer sat opposite to put in her two cents. "I'm the only one left now," she said in a small voice.

When she began to cry he ordered a slice of cake for her, and when she took the first bite he asked if she could remember them having rabbits during the war. Aunt Ellen remembered

it well, but they all got sick from some disease, she said. He nodded, and Aunt Ellen got into a fluster about who was paying for the cake, and then it turned out she couldn't eat it anyway. Afterward he took her home. She wanted to hold his hand all the way, and when the street door closed behind her he stood outside staring at it.

Grandmother died when he was twenty-five, so his memories of her are clear. When he was growing up, his mother and Aunt Ellen would sometimes leave him with Grandmother and go to the movies together. Memories can cover each other up, but he especially remembers one time he went over to her place with some leftovers of Aunt Ellen's. She was going to give him a cookie, just as she always did, but first she needed to go to the bathroom. She went herself, but when she was there she called for him. She said that because she was old she could no longer reach. He wiped her, and as he did so there came a small sound from inside her. It made him look at her, and the way she looked back at him made him drop the toilet paper into the bowl. He told her she could pull up her underwear by herself. But she couldn't.

"I've nothing on under my dress," she said.

He helped her into the living room and sat her down in the chair where she always sat. Then he laid a blanket over her bare legs. He asked her when the home help was coming. But the home help had already been, his grandmother told him, and reached for a cookie.

She had that look in her eye. The look Aunt Ellen and his mother always talked about before turning away, and he remembers how he hung around the soccer fields for a long time before going home. When he got back, his mother and Aunt

Ellen were in the kitchen smoking cigarettes and they asked him how Grandmother was. He said she was fine and she sent her love. He sat there at the end of the table, and afterward he stood as he always did, together with his mother, and waved across the lawn to Aunt Ellen who stood at her window and waved back. It wouldn't pay to tell. His mother didn't care for Grandmother, and yet she was always tagging along behind her. Every day, week in and week out, through one story after another. Mother and Aunt Ellen tagging along.

One of the episodes his mother and Aunt Ellen talked about most often as an example of how unreasonable Grandmother was concerned one Sunday during the war when his mother and Aunt Ellen had spent all day making paper cuttings. It was one of the stories he had heard told the most and they told it in exactly the same way. It was about how they had been cutting all day until the tips of their fingers were red and sore. Then they had put all their fine paper cuttings onto a string and joined them together in an intricate pattern to make a mobile. They hung the mobile up above the dining table, only for the two brothers who had yet to leave home to get the idea of using it as a target. His mother and Aunt Ellen tried to get Grandmother to make them stop, but all she did was sit with her coffee cup raised to her mouth and giggle.

"She giggled?" he asked.

"Yes, she damn well did."

And he imagined how Grandmother had sat there with a sugar cube between her teeth, observing her daughters with amusement as they ran around the table in tears.

Later, Grandmother died, and now his mother too, and he was over forty and Aunt Ellen had looked like a frail bird in the

doorway when he took her home after the funeral. It wasn't enough to close the circle, he thought to himself as he crossed over the lawns between the buildings to take the back stairs up to his place. The apartment felt empty. He thought about his mother as he sat in the kitchen waiting for the coffee to brew. She had still seemed alert enough, and he remembered how everything around her got so infected at the end. It was like she had been leaking. Maybe it was the cancer, but he thought she smelled sour, and she felt around with her hands. All the time, back and forth over the duvet, her fingers like stalks. She told him all kinds of little stories. How he had bitten her when he was small. How she regretted not having moved farther away. She told him about his grandfather, and how she loved to follow him around as a child and watch him as he sealed the potato sacks. Grandfather talked to the cows when he gave them fodder and washed their udders. Grandfather kept rabbits at the back of the cowshed. They were white and brown, and bred well during the war.

She didn't want him to go. He had to stay at her side. Every time he got up to stretch his legs she became uneasy. Eventually he lay down beside her.

That was when it came out. How she and Aunt Ellen had come home from school one day and Grandmother had been standing at the entrance of the cowshed. She was in Grandfather's gray milking apron and said they were to follow her in. As soon as they passed the cows and came to the back of the shed, Grandmother opened the gate of the rabbit enclosure. She said the rabbits had gotten sick with disease. The rabbits hopped around in the straw and Grandmother chased one of the brown ones into a corner. She took hold of

the scruff of its neck and pressed it against her chest to make its legs stop kicking.

"This is how it's done," she said, and without wanting to watch, Mother and Aunt Ellen saw Grandmother's hand squeeze the air out of the rabbit.

It peed on the apron while it happened, and a long, thin sound came out of Aunt Ellen. Mother wanted to jump on Grandmother and make her stop. She was going to scratch her. Or else she was going to run, or maybe just scream. But she did none of those things, because Grandmother looked at her in such a strange way. Like it was a kind of experiment and the idea was to find out how much chaos she could cause inside her. The more chaos and noise she could make there, the better.

"And I just stood there all quiet. I stood there and watched as though I didn't care, while Aunt Ellen ran away and Grandmother squeezed the life out of four more rabbits. When she was done, her hands were shaking and there was such a wild look in her eyes. She said I was to go inside and wash."

He held his mother's hand as she told the story. She looked at him with childlike eyes and claimed the cancer had come from that moment when in order for Grandmother not to win she had refused to be affected by the evil thing she did. He nodded, because what was he supposed to say? And then she was dead, placed inside the casket and buried, and he had packed away most of her stuff, but not all. There are still a number of boxes, the bags for the Salvation Army, and above the kitchen sink the obituary notice he reads every time he washes his hands.

# SHE FREQUENTED CEMETERIES

SHE STARTED FREQUENTING CEMETERIES THAT SUMMER, preferring the ones others rarely visited. She could go straight from social events with white wine, canapés, and peripheral acquaintances, cycle to the nearest cemetery, and find the corner where no one ever really went. At the far end of Vestre Cemetery, by the Inuit and the Faeroese and the war graves, down by the disused chapel was a quiet spot. Well away from the plots where brewers, publishers, and prime ministers lay shoulder to shoulder and were dead. There was no edged grass, no small ponds with specially purchased ducks. Most of all, it resembled the hinterland of Jutland, depopulated and with plywood boards across the windows, and through it all a diagonal tunnel of willow trees. No one ever went there, so that was where she liked to go. In the same way, she was fond of the Jewish cemetery and the Catholic cemetery, and, provided she chose the right times and the right spots, Assistens Cemetery could be quiet, too.

Her favorite, though, was just between Frederiksberg and Valby. It was best in the twilight. In late July the evenings were still long and the place was like an overgrown park. Walking along the paths in the cemetery she found the unkempt graves

of long-forgotten painters and poets, and at the northern end she came across a section where roses grew everywhere. The bushes had grown over the stones, weeds had tangled up in them, and they were the same roses her mother had at home. Pink, with small flowers, and no one bothered to cut them back. When she got to this part of the cemetery she would stroll peacefully around the paths as if she was drawing arabesques with her feet.

She was thirty-five years old and that summer she was avoiding her girlfriends. Now and then they would call her and ask about meeting up, but she would decline whenever possible. She knew they would be troubled by her situation, and that her way of dealing with what she claimed had happened would excite them and cause them to speculate impulsively. On a few occasions she tried to explain the situation to them, but it had not been pleasant. A few of them had tried to talk her out of it, suggesting her condition was the result of loneliness or biology. One had interrogated her. Was she quite sure, was it wise, wouldn't it be better if . . . All of them wanted to give her advice, even if she didn't need any. She knew why she was going to the cemeteries, why she continued to walk back and forth, and around and about, eating ice cream and rolling rose petals between her fingers. She was waiting, and while she was waiting she was putting something behind her and trying to find a new way of looking at the future. She walked slowly and if not devoutly then at least pensively and with a sense for the little things she didn't feel she'd noticed for years. She saw the wild cats that lived in the bushes. She saw how they drank water from the pond in the middle of the cemetery. She saw the magpie's young and the graves that had fallen in and

the gravestones that had tipped over so it looked like the dead and their monuments were about to change places. As summer passed she saw the plants grow and fade, and some evenings she would pick a few of the pink roses and take them home with her to put in a vase on the bedside table. She thought mostly about how hard it was to be allowed to believe that good would arrive and how things would be when in spite of everything it did.

What had happened wasn't exactly spectacular. She had met a man. That was all. She loved him, and the way she loved him had made her settle into a place inside her where intangible things took on natural substance. She felt at home there and she knew that at some point she would look back on this summer as the one when she stopped holding back. Her feelings were strong and reciprocated. She sensed it, yet she knew also it would take time before they could be together. He was in mourning for things he'd lost, and his mourning was unhurried. She could see that when he looked up at her from the table. But she was all right with it, because when he looked at her she was in no doubt and could abandon herself to the hope that he would bring all the good with him when he came.

But there was no way she could explain this to her girlfriends. They demanded evidence. They wanted to know who had died, why he kept crying, and if it really wasn't just his own fault. They wanted to know if she'd looked into him and if she knew what laying down arms involved. She mustn't get her heart broken, they said. That was the important thing. Not to get her heart broken. And all the time they jumped from floe to floe with their dreams of disappearing into the current, losing control, abandoning themselves. Always trying to fill

in the empty spaces and keep things moving in the meantime. Doing their best to avoid going home too early to their little apartments that reminded them of coffee bars and bus shelters every time they stepped through the door. Love, nothing less. That was what they wanted. That was what they craved, unconditionally. It was what they talked about when they put their arms under hers and dragged her through the parks, as though the parks were eyes in a storm that had to be sat out, and now she had found it. But she couldn't tell them. There was no way she could share it with them, so that summer she frequented cemeteries.

She would focus on her job, including her hospitality duties, but when it was done she would get on her bike and be gone. In the early evening she would pass through the iron gates into Park Cemetery, stroll past the dead painters, the poets, and head for the place where the pink roses were. When she got there she would walk between the graves, and as she went she closed her eyes to the parts of reality the others were keeping a watch on and imagined the man, who could only be with her in spirit, lacing his fingers in hers. They would walk there in various scenarios, sometimes silently, but together. They would be walking there when he said he loved her. Things like that would be said as they walked side by side through the cemeteries in the various stages of their as-yet-uninitiated time together. She had no trouble picturing the man zigzagging in between the small plots with a child on his shoulders. She could see the man and the child leap out from among the bushes where the wild cats lived. She could feel him kiss her behind the cemetery toilets, see the child fall and hurt itself, hear the wheels of the buggy squeak. Often he would sit down on one

of the benches a little farther on and pat the space beside him so she would sit there with him, and that was what she did.

There was nothing secretive about it. She was in love with someone, and while it was going on she thought about the good that had happened and the good that was going to happen. The noise of traffic on Søndre Fasanvej and Roskildevej remained a distant hum as she stole names for the child from the gravestones, and it felt nice, the same way it felt nice to let her thoughts sink into the earth where one day they themselves would lie, white through to the bone and tangled up in each other while the world carried on above them. That was okay, she thought. That kind of death was a good thing, and she would tell him that when he came, and she would tell the child when it was old enough, and perhaps a particularly distraught girlfriend one day. Until then she would keep it to herself, frequent the cemeteries, waiting and occasionally squatting down to see the cats stretch their necks toward the water.

# THE WADDEN SEA

WHEN I THINK BACK ON FANØ, IT'S MOSTLY OF THE Wadden Sea and the many shipmaster cottages. In the spring-time the oyster-catcher would fly low over the thatched roofs, and I would go down to the tide pole to see how high above my head the water would have come if I'd been there in 1852. Sønderho, where I lived, was beautiful, even if they did call it the World's End. There were many artists and musicians living in that little community. There were rich people too, though I didn't know any of them, and then there were the locals and the town alcoholics. Like rooks, they tended to attract each other so that certain parts of the town were clusters of people with indistinct pronunciation and chinking shopping bags. Those are the kinds of things I remember, and also the multiallergic woman riding around the little lanes and unpaved roads on that wheelchair-*cum*-scooter of hers. Rumor had it she could predict people's futures, and she wore a mask over her face. From the mask a tube went down to a machine that provided her with oxygen and at the same time filtered impurities from the air. She looked like a UFO that had landed on Earth and had found a way of getting around. Like a lot of other people in Sønderho, she was from Copenhagen. She had moved to Sønderho because the area's sparse vegetation made the air purer, and because

it's good for the sick that the Wadden Sea is like one big, moist lung.

It was because of Sønderho's genuine feel, its unspoiled surroundings, and the healthy outdoor life that we moved there. My mother was an actress and had worked a few jobs before being struck by a kind of depression that put a stop to everything. We lived in a two-room apartment in Nørrebro, just the two of us, and it was hard for me to cope, especially on the weekends. I persuaded Mom to visit the doctor and he gave her some pills that didn't help. It was a lady with long, flowing robes who convinced Mom that Sønderho was a good place to work on her depression, or *fear of life,* as they decided to call it. Mom was becoming more reliant on her medication. She needed deliverance so she canceled the lease on the apartment. We had to get away from everything artificial. Copenhagen was one big fabrication, she said. She was going to find herself, and I went with her.

She rented a house in Sønderho and hoped the clean air might help her get off the medication that fear of life was craving. And she actually did start feeling a whole lot better quite quickly and went around the sparsely furnished house teaching me to say the words *pristine, Frisian,* and *Netherlandic.* Shortly after, she enrolled me in the school and herself in the local citizens' association. Things were working out, and I would go running around the narrow lanes in town, looking in the windows with their porcelain dogs that sat looking out. Or else I would hide behind the garden fences. On Sundays we ate stewed apples with macaroons and whipped cream at the neighbor's. Mom found friends, and at the local inn she became smitten with folk dance and the story about lacing

the coffee with Brøndums Snaps because Rød Aalborg was for mainlanders.

And that was how fear of life after only a short time managed to get on the train from Copenhagen to Esbjerg. It turned out able to sail on the ferry too, and then it got on the bus for Sønderho and rode the nine miles from the ferry to the World's End. Someone must have given it the address, because it came right to our house and knocked on the door, and it was the kind of visitor who puts a foot in the door, barges in, and refuses to leave. It crawled into bed with my mother and went to the store for new supplies each day and then shut itself in and piled itself up in the shed so that after a few months I had to call my grandmother.

I could tell Grandma was shaken up standing there amid all that medication out in the shed. She asked me how I could get my bike out without upsetting everything. I could tell she knew fear of life, and I could tell she knew it was a kind of fear that took in the whole of people's lives and could make them forsaken wherever in the world. She was on the verge of crying, but she couldn't, because it was my turn now to be small, so instead she stayed with us for a month. While Grandma was with us, she sat with my mother a lot and talked with her about the future and how we had to have one, and she walked me to school and sewed new covers for the chairs in the living room. After a while she got Mom eating and pulled me aside in the kitchen and said all things would pass in time.

She was right about all things passing in time, because Mom got better, so Grandma went home again. I could have gone with her, but I wouldn't, because for one thing, Mom was

trying to get into some good daily habits, and for another, she was having notions that the Wadden Sea had healing power. Anything that came into contact with the Wadden Sea was connected to that power. The notion made her get up early in the mornings, and it made her put on her gumboots and her overcoat. She would go down to the beach and look for fossilized sea urchins, and when she came home she would put them under her pillow. She found shells and made holes in them for turning them into mobiles. She twined dreamcatchers, fixed crab claws and dried seaweed to them, and hung them up over our beds. Everything had to be authentic, she said. It was artificiality that destroyed everything.

Almost every day she went down to the Wadden Sea and almost every day I went with her. We would walk along the unpaved road from Sønderho to the beach, and sometimes we met the multiallergic woman, whose breathing problems were especially bad in the wintertime. She would be sitting under a big rain cape, and Mom would be funny and say, *Here comes the pyramid tent.*

One particularly cold and heavy day in February we met her just like that on our way out to the Wadden Sea. She had the mask over her mouth and a pair of big orange glasses just above it, so it looked as if she was wearing a visor. Her wheelchair was a mass of tubes and gadgets that made her alien in her surroundings. I could hear machines wheezing and pulling, and I could see how her fingers controlled the switches and joysticks while Mom was talking. Mom was talking about how she wanted to learn to make lace and how she had discovered the coordinates of what she called the Wadden Sea Void. The multiallergic woman listened, and while Mom

explained I looked at the woman's peculiar craft, which I'd also seen could ride over dunes. When I looked up I saw I'd been caught in the woman's gaze above her mouth mask. Her eyes sank into mine, and I couldn't look away because of her eyes, which filled up the orange glasses completely. I can't say why, but I think she knew. Sometimes you change things you remember when you know what happened later, but what happened was that Mom and I carried on our way.

We scrambled over the reeds that lay stacked in bundles on the other side of the dike and went down onto the beach. We walked through the fillet of crushed razor shells and out onto the wet sand. After we'd walked for a while, Mom started looking for small splinters of amber on the tide line. While she looked, I stood with my hands in my pockets watching the Germans farther up the beach. They were flying kites and parachutes, or squatting in the washed-up seaweed as though they'd just gotten out of their cars to pee, and I felt removed from them.

When we'd gone farther out into the Wadden Sea, Mom asked me if I knew where the Wadden Sea ended and began. The Wadden Sea is always shifting, but in the summer it was easy to tell the difference between land and sea. In summer the weather was fine and the breakers would be clearly visible, but in winter it was harder. One can get helplessly lost in the Wadden Sea. The local children knew, just like children in Sweden know that one can get lost in the forests, and children from inland Jutland have all heard about the great void that exists at the center of the rye fields. At certain times of day the Wadden Sea is like a big, wet sheet of gray cardboard that you couldn't cover with block letters even if you had the rest

of your life. Everyone knew that, yet Mom stood there poking her finger into it.

I said to her that we mustn't forget to go back in. She said there was a place where you went from the artificial world into a life-giving zone. This was the Wadden Sea Void. That was the place we had to find, and she had the coordinates: a diagonal from Ribe Cathedral down through Mandø Island up to Sønderho and back again to the cathedral. It was a triangle like the one off Bermuda. Somewhere inside it, everything artificial about us would be taken away and what remained would be our essential selves.

We walked for a long time looking for the place. When we could no longer see the dunes, a bank of fog came and settled around us. I think we stopped going straight and started going in circles. Mom was in front, and I was behind her and lost my bearings and didn't know what was inside or what was out. I looked for the kites, the parachutes, and the Germans, but saw nothing. I looked to see the direction the birds were flying, but it seemed random. All I wanted were warm, dry socks and gumboots, or my bed. After a while, Mom stopped and stood still with her back half-turned to me. She stood there with her eyes closed and her hair down. Then she pointed into the fog. She pointed into it like it was a piece of psychology. She said the Wadden Sea was an image in the mind's eye, and that she was glad I wanted to go with her into it.

## AUTHOR'S ACKNOWLEDGMENTS

I wish to thank the Danish Arts Council and the Danish Arts Agency for supporting this book with grants, and writer Knud Sørensen and the Danish Center for Writers and Translators at Hald Hovedgaard for housing me during the writing. Thanks to Julie Paludan-Müller, Brigid Hughes, Fiona McCrae, Fiona Maazel, and other book people and writers in the United States and Denmark who cheered and boosted me as I went along. A special thanks to my working partner, translator Martin Aitken. And last but not least: thank you to my family and friends.

## TRANSLATOR'S ACKNOWLEDGMENTS

Thanks to Brigid Hughes and Fiona McCrae for their intrepid publishing, to the Danish Arts Council for its generous support, to Dorthe Nors for her magnificent stories and seamless collaboration—and to my son, Gustav, for such tireless good cheer.

# PUSHKIN PRESS

Pushkin Press was founded in 1997, and publishes novels, essays, memoirs, children's books—everything from timeless classics to the urgent and contemporary.

Our books represent exciting, high-quality writing from around the world: we publish some of the twentieth century's most widely acclaimed, brilliant authors such as Stefan Zweig, Marcel Aymé, Antal Szerb, Paul Morand and Yasushi Inoue, as well as compelling and award-winning contemporary writers, including Andrés Neuman, Edith Pearlman and Ryu Murakami.

Pushkin Press publishes the world's best stories, to be read and read again. For more amazing stories, visit www.pushkinpress.com.

# PUSHKIN PRESS

Pushkin Press was founded in 1997, and publishes novels, essays, memoirs, children's books—everything from timeless classics to the urgent and contemporary.

Our books represent exciting, high-quality writing from around the world: we publish some of the twentieth century's most widely acclaimed, brilliant authors such as Stefan Zweig, Marcel Aymé, Antal Szerb, Paul Morand and Yasushi Inoue, as well as compelling and award-winning contemporary writers, including Andrés Neuman, Edith Pearlman and Ryu Murakami.

Pushkin Press publishes the world's best stories, to be read and read again. For more amazing stories, visit www.pushkinpress.com.